Violet's Roots

By Taylor Painter

Published by Forget Me Not Romances, an imprint of Winged Publications

ISBN-13:978-1-968792-06-0

Prologue

It's been two years since Blaire Whitfield found the mysterious diary at an antique store while shopping for farmhouse decor. In the midst of the most depressing season of her life, Blaire was offered comfort through the words written in the mystifying diary belonging to the wonderfully eccentric midwife named Addie. Through Addie's deepest thoughts about childbirth, life on her farm, and grief after loss, Blaire began to feel joy for the first time since her father passed away.

During the time that Blaire prepared to move into the beautiful old farmhouse she had just bought, she was also swept off her feet by a handsome police officer named Joseph, while working at her nursing job. Things started to look up for the despondent young woman who mourned the loss of her loved ones and longed for the peace she felt only during her childhood years.

It wasn't until the day Blaire moved into the farmhouse with the help of Joseph, that Addie was revealed as Ms. Adelaide, the patient Blaire had once cared for at the nursing home. In addition to this stunning revelation, Blaire also uncovered the most profound piece of the story…Blaire was moving into Addie's old home. The one from which she'd written every word in the diary Blaire regarded as treasure.

In an unsettling confirmation, a ghostly apparition described at Ms. Adelaide was seen by Joseph outside the farmhouse, embracing an oblivious Blaire. Though completely horrified, Blaire ultimately overcame the fears that made a vigorous effort to steal her newfound joy. Now, with what she feels like is Addie's daily guidance that assists her along, Blaire navigates her new life with the realization that wonders never cease.

"Budding"

ONE

The days are long and heavy, dripping with a sultriness that only a southern summer can deliver. The air is thick with both warmth and floral aromas. The fruits of labor are abundant, in regard to both crops and babies.

As I relax on the old porch swing in the solace of a balmy evening, a gentle breeze combs through my hair - the faintest tease. The bullfrogs are beginning to croak from the hidden creek. The cicadas sound their evening calls as the day fades into twilight. The hens are starting, one by one, to retire to the safety of their roosts. Ginger, my mama-cow, is resting in the old barn with her brand-new calf.

This morning at dawn, I faced the eastern window as I brewed myself a maple latte. A new day's sunlight emerged over the dale and flooded the kitchen. I'd considered myself on "baby watch" for the past week, *trying not to be away from home for any longer than absolutely necessary. As my coffee perked, I peered out toward the barn. It was then that I became aware Ginger would deliver the calf very soon, as she went from lying to standing, lying to standing.*

Abandoning the percolator on the stove, I shoved my feet into my rubber garden boots by the door. Then, carefully closing the screen door behind me, I quietly strode across the porch. I crossed the yard slowly and approached Ginger from behind, observing discreetly. The baby's front hooves and nose were beginning to emerge as Ginger's large body heaved and pushed. I smiled at the sight, satisfied that Ginger wouldn't deliver the calf during the hottest part of the day.

The robins whistled their melody, the perfect accompaniment to the timeless, sacred event that was taking place just beyond the pasture gate. The beginning of a new life emerged effortlessly and beautifully, an almost evocative feeling washing over me as I felt the power of divine creation.

As the fog hovered over the earth, the golden sunrise shining through it, the wet calf exited Ginger's swollen rear and fell swiftly to the earth. The new mother immediately turned and began licking her young, who was already beginning to wiggle around on the dew-covered grass. A beautiful, blonde-colored baby, like her Charolais father.

Quiet, warm tears wet my cheeks as I watched the miracle of life begin before me, once again. Ginger lovingly kissed her new baby, paying no attention to me as I stood just on the other side of the fence. Soon, the furry, damp calf clumsily rose to its hind feet. Stumbling and falling a few times, it finally managed to stand on all fours and wobbled weakly to its mother's full udder.

As it nursed, frothy white milk dripping from its mouth, I observed that the baby was a little bull calf, and I marveled at the sight of natural instinct as the newborn knew just what to do. No interventions necessary, no instructions, no instruments. Just perfectly orchestrated birth, in its purest form.

There was an audible hush that fell over the farm in those moments. Other than the sound of the birds singing - perhaps a song of celebration - there was only a peaceful silence. Even the writing spider sat perfectly still in her dew-spotted web she'd woven on the wire fence. It seemed as if that moment was just carved out and sat right before me to enjoy in awe.

I walked back onto the porch, smiling over my shoulder as I opened the screen door and stepped inside the house. The smell of freshly brewed coffee and the sound of it bubbling in the pot added a warm layer to my delight as I entered my dear home.

It was then that I heard my phone ringing from the kitchen counter. I quickly strode across the hardwoods and picked it up, to see that it was Laura, one of my expectant mothers. I'd been waiting for her call.

She said that her pains were coming regularly and were rather intense. I swiftly gathered all of my supplies, including jars of homemade broth and grapefruit switchel for Laura to drink, and I took my coffee to-go.

I smile now, thinking of how two births occurred in my presence today, before the pale blue morning glories even closed their blossoms.

Laura's labor quickly picked up the pace after I'd arrived at her beautiful country cabin. There was no time for switchel or honey or even a back massage. As soon as I'd walked through the front door and into Laura's small kitchen, I heard the groans that told me it would not be long before we'd meet the baby.

I quickly but calmly examined Laura and made the decision not to unpack all of my supplies. Instead, I took a pair of rubber gloves from my bag and prepared to catch the baby, as he was surely coming soon.

Laura groaned low and deep, involuntary grunts rising up from within her powerful body. She rocked back and forth on her hands and knees by the living room loveseat as the bulge of the baby's crown appeared at her bottom.

Just as I had with Ginger, only an hour prior, I observed the birth intently but without disturbing the mother or the infant. I was prepared to assist, if necessary, but my involvement was not needed. Instead, both mothers seemingly effortlessly birthed their babies just as their bodies were designed to do.

At the sound of the first cry, a magical sense of wonder floated around us, hovering most heavily over Laura and the newborn, as she held him to her chest and shushed away his cry. All those present were blanketed by the deep, heart-filling, soul-enchanting lull that seems to mystify time. The transient "golden hour" with the new baby seems like only seconds, and as fleeting as if it were.

Laura had given birth three times before, and each of her children were there to witness the miracle - a homeschool lesson, no doubt. Both she and the baby were positively perfect when I left them wrapped in each other's warmth and came home to check on the farm and prepare for tomorrow's visit.

I'll return to Laura before noon with another half gallon of broth, a garden-fresh frittata with eggs from my pastured hens, and a warm orzo casserole. Once at Laura's cabin, I will prepare a hot tea of fresh ginger and orange peels as the new mother relaxes in bed with the little one.

I'll then offer to hold the baby and examine him while she eats and drinks to her utmost satisfaction, staying close enough for her to reach out and touch us if she so desires.

It's been a deeply satisfying day, drenched in happiness and droplets of sweat and tears. As I sit in the balmy, still air, the weight of the miraculous day falls upon me, and I feel nearly ready for sleep. After a golden saffron latte, of course. I'm unsure if tomorrow can compare, but I'm optimistic.

You'll hear about it.

Addie

TWO

The wind howls outside the frosted windows, sending frigid air and misty rain against the farmhouse. The house pops and groans as another gust whips through. I close the diary and rise from my warm spot on the couch. Dill doesn't budge an inch as I pass by him, lying on the floor in front of the *Fisher Mama Bear*. It could use another chunk of wood.

I flip the porch light on and pull aside the blue plaid curtain that covers the small window in the front door. I peer out at the bare trees, their limbs bending in the miserably cold wind. I'm grateful to be in a warm house with a pot full of potato soup on the stovetop.

Joseph's patrol car stops on the gravel driveway, finally home from a long day's work. Dill rises and slowly pads across the floor to join me by the door. "Daddy's home," I coo as I rub his soft ears. He wags his tail at the news.

Crossing the living room again and into the kitchen, I grab two bowls from the cabinet and set them on the dining table.

Although Joseph and I have just celebrated our first wedding anniversary, I still get giddy each time I set the table for more than one. I don't imagine I'll ever grow tired of it, and I'm still in disbelief at the thought that I'm not alone anymore.

The candlestick on the table flickers the glowing light of invitation alongside the fresh bread and golden butter.

It's hard to believe it's been two years since I found Addie's diary inside that old, thrifted nightstand that now sits by our bed; perhaps the same exact spot where it started out. The realization that Addie wrote many of the words in her diaries from this very room is surreal. I can almost feel her looking over my shoulder and encouraging me to press on when I'm trying something new in the kitchen. Her kitchen. My kitchen. *Our* kitchen.

Each time I wipe down the scarred wooden countertops, I think of the many times Addie must've done the same. Her tiny vases of fresh flowers sat in the windowsill above the sink where we've shared the dishwashing duties, though at different times. The scuffed hardwood floors have supported the weight of countless steps as Addie strode across them, tending the home in the solace of these very walls, or scurrying to gather her bag of supplies when suddenly called to another birthing.

Interrupting my daydreams is the familiar sound of Joseph entering through the front door.

"Hey!" I call, as I carefully place two spoons on the table.

Joseph flashes a wide grin as he locks the door behind him.

"Hey, there. It sure smells good in here," he drawls.

"Potato soup and fresh bread." I beam as he crosses the living room toward me.

It's taken some genuine effort, but I've improved my cooking skills immensely with Addie's help.

"That sounds awesome. It's cold out there," Joseph says with a shiver.

"Miserably cold. I went out to check on the chickens this evening, and I ran back inside as fast as I could."

Joseph knows how much I hate winters. The whole season, I long for the warmth and vibrancy that summer brings, when everything is plump and ripe and beautiful. I find myself wishing for the days when I can swing open the screen door and pad barefoot across the porch on my way to cut a bunch of fresh zinnias. Or gather eggs and tomatoes as the hummingbirds flit around the farmhouse. The only thing I can find the least bit comforting about these winter months are the memories the chilly air sometimes brings.

As a cold wind sweeps through the yard with the smell of the wood burning in the stove, I can almost see Daddy in his plaid flannel shirt, chopping firewood. Or my grandmama making pumpkin pies and casseroles, her knit sweater worn over her favorite pink apron.

Before I found this place, and Joseph, and Addie, I spent my winters in a shell of a body, in a shell of a house – not even a home, but merely a space where I bathed, slept, and indulged in true crime TV, fast food, and synthetic vitamin D supplements. I'd stomp back and forth to work, shut myself in and feel sorry for myself until Spring…when I'd feel only slightly less miserable.

But then, my joy was miraculously restored for the first time since my Daddy died. Thanks to Addie's guidance through both her diaries and perennial flowers that sprout up voluntarily; and of course, Joseph, who happened into my life on an ordinary day at work. It didn't take long for me to realize that I wanted Joseph in my life permanently, and it fortunately didn't take him long to decide the same, because he proposed after three months of dating. I excitedly accepted with all of my heart.

"How was your day?" Joseph asks as he pulls me into a tight embrace.

"Nice and relaxing," I answer as my mind replays the day's events.

Stretching and folding the gooey ball of bread dough in the morning. Pulling on my hoodie and rubber boots and going out to feed the chickens. Making the bed and washing the dishes, the clinking of glasses and silverware trying to fill the empty home. Shaping and baking the bread in the afternoon while Dill slept on the rug by my feet. Folding afghans and draping them over the furniture, only to unfold them later when I'd settled onto the couch to read Addie's diary while I sipped a warm latte.

On the bookshelf in our bedroom are six other diaries belonging to Addie, one of those being a hand-written recipe book rather than a diary, but holding as much value as the diaries themselves. It's where I found the instructions for making things like homemade bread, bone broth, gnocchi, yogurt, and herbal tinctures. I must admit that although I grew up in the kitchen with my Grandmama, our style was making biscuits from Crisco vegetable shortening and spreading Country Crock margarine onto a slice of toasted Wonder Bread.

I am currently reading the sixth diary of the seven and savoring it as slowly as possible. I allow myself no more than one chapter per day in the winter months; if I didn't limit myself, I would have devoured every word long ago and I just can't bear to close this sweet reprieve that I've been enchanted by in the last two years. The final diary, covered with hundreds of orange and black fluttering butterflies, lies in wait as I inch my way toward full indulgence.

Until the ground thaws and I can exhale relief into the warm air around me, I will live vicariously through

Addie's words of sweet summers' past. I can vividly imagine each scene as described from right here on the most heavenly place on Earth.

"Let's eat," I take Joseph's hand and pull him gently behind me.

"Anything exciting happen today?" I ask as I fill our bowls with the steamy soup.

"Nothing to write home about." Joseph snickers. "I gave a couple citations. Nothing major."

I always ask about his day, but I don't pry for too many details because I know that once he's off duty, he doesn't like to think about work very much.

"Well, I'm glad you're home now. I worry about you out there; people are crazy," I reply.

"Oh, how well I know," he agrees with widened eyes.

Taking my seat across from him at our small dining table, I glance around to make sure we have everything we need and sigh with satisfaction.

"This has got to be one of my favorite parts of the whole day," I declare.

"Well, I enjoy mealtimes myself," he replies with a grin.

I roll my eyes. "Not just the food, goofy. Sitting here with you is what I mean."

"I'm teasing ya," he says with a wink. "Me too."

"I've got a lot to be thankful for, you know," I reply.

As I say the words, I can feel the thrills of gratitude bubbling up inside me.

"We *both* have a lot to be thankful for," Joseph says between laps of steamy soup.

I don't know what I ever did to deserve him, but I found a diamond in the rough with Joseph. He's kind and gentle, yet strong and protective. He's everything I always hoped for, but never thought I'd find.

I assumed I'd be lonely forever, retiring from *Sunny Meadows Home & Rehab,* having nobody but my best friend Jill to see me through life's downs and ultra downs. But, the only thing that hasn't changed yet is that I'm still working at "The Home". As swiftly as Joseph came into my life, Jill moved away to the mountains of Virginia to live by her husband's ailing father, where they'll inherit his estate once he passes. It was as if the transition was perfectly orchestrated in that Joseph took over Jill's role of my personal confidante. The week following the day that she stood beside me as my Matron of Honor, she broke the news to me that she was leaving.

I miss Jill terribly; but we keep in touch as much as we can. I keep her up to date on the patients she once cared for at The Home, which is a bittersweet reminder of her life here in North Carolina. I joke that it was harder for her to leave her patients than it was to leave me - her best friend. And I'm still not totally convinced that's not true.

Tomorrow morning will find me clocking in for another shift. Though I love my patients, what was once my only true joy has become the least desirable part of my life. I'm not quite sure if it has to do with Jill being gone, or the contrast between it and my new home life when the two are compared. Maybe a little bit of both.

THREE

"Good morning!" I greet Sharon as I step into the small, dusty nurses' station. The familiar wall-papered room, adorned with heavy old furniture and antique wall sconces welcomes me back in.

"How was the night?" I ask.

From the looks of her, it didn't go well. Sharon looks absolutely worn out.

"It was okay," she answers weakly, fumbling to sort some pieces of paperwork.

"Mrs. Deese fell at six o'clock," she continues.

I know this incident has thrown a wrench in Sharon's whole morning. Six o'clock is when the night shift nurses are right in the middle of passing out Prilosec and Synthroid tablets to every single patient that resides at Sunny Meadows.

"Is she hurt?" I ask.

"She doesn't appear to be. But I've started her on the head trauma protocol just in case."

"Since she's on Aspirin," she adds.

I can't imagine going a full day here without a patient falling; sadly, it just comes with the territory, no matter what type of preventative measures are in place.

"What do you have left to do?" I ask.

"I still have to call the family, finish the incident report, and then do the rest of my charting," Sharon replies.

"Let me clock in real quick, and I'll help you."

I exit the small, dim nurses' station and round the corner to the time clock. 7 o' clock sharp, it reads.

"Hey, hey!" Cindy chirps as she approaches the time clock, carrying her gigantic satchel and thirty-ounce plastic cup full of sweet tea.

I enjoy working with Cindy, caring for the patients on the 200-wing. Her chipper mood and almost-overwhelming personality always seems to make the time pass more quickly.

"Good morning!" I reply with a grin before darting back into the nurses' station to join Sharon.

"I'll call Mrs. Deese's granddaughter," I say as I re-enter the quaint, dim quarters.

I grab the thick plastic chart from the table, where Sharon has already placed it. I flip the cover and take the contact information page before rolling in the swivel chair over to the phone hanging on the wall above the desk.

"Tina?" I ask as she sleepily answers the call.

I inform her of her grandmother's fall from bed this morning to which she groggily replies, "Okay. Bye."

"Well…that's done," I say to Sharon as I fill in the granddaughter's name on the incident report sheet.

"She was a ray of sunshine, too," I mumble.

Once Sharon has clocked out and the residents of the 100-wing are my full responsibility, I begin the repetitive "med pass" where I assume my position as a glorified, legal drug dealer. The patients are happy to see me as I darken their door with the little cup full of pills. Most of them are, anyway.

After filling my cart with the juices and puddings I'll need to help administer the innumerable amount of medications, I head down the dark hallway and flip on the overhead lights. Meg will be helping me today; she's around here somewhere, helping the residents get ready for the day. I know without a doubt that we're all in good hands when Meg is on duty.

No sooner than I finish giving Mr. Silvers his morning insulin shot, I hear one of the most dreaded sounds that a nurse can hear. (Other than complete silence followed by someone commenting, "It sure is *quiet*." The "Q-word" is forbidden, as most people in the healthcare field know.)

"*Nurse! N-u-u-u-u-r-s-e!*" Mrs. Timmons yells from her room at the end of the long hallway. I slam the medicine cart drawer shut and jog down the hall, aware that she could need help locating her TV remote, have fallen and broken a hip, or anything in between. You just never know.

Upon racing into her room, I find her sitting on the edge of her bed, pointing toward the bed next to hers… the bed belonging to Mrs. White.

"Is she alright?" Mrs. Timmons asks with a look of bewilderment. "She don't look right," she says of Mrs. White, who is lying on her back and looking up at the ceiling.

I immediately realize that Mrs. Timmons' concern is valid as I rush over to Mrs. White's bed and check her limp, clammy wrist for a pulse. I stare down at her still, fixed eyes and note her blue-tinged opened mouth.

I drop her wrist. "Cindy!" I yell, exiting the room and running for the 'crash cart' which is stashed away in the corner of the nurses' station.

Cindy rushes out of her patients' room and looks at me with wide eyes as I race down the hall.

"Code status on Mable White!" I yell as I sprint.

Cindy bounds across the intersection of the hallways and rapidly flips through the documents I've left on my medicine cart.

"Full code!" she shouts, as I round the corner pushing the bulky cart full of emergency supplies. I knew it.

Back in the patients' room, Cindy has already pulled the privacy curtain that separates the two ladies and has begun chest compressions as I break the zip ties off the drawer and fling it open.

"Here, let's roll her," I say, holding up an orange plastic board by its handle.

Together, we roll Mrs. White onto her back and place the board beneath her before rolling her onto her back again.

"Meg!" I yell, pushing the button on the call light cord and then letting it fall to the floor.

"Meg?" I call again as I place the rubber Ambu bag over Mrs. White's mouth and nose. I know Meg must be nearby.

Cindy continues chest compressions as she counts under her breath. I lightly wince at the sound of cracking ribs as I fumble around the curtain for Mrs. Timmons' night-time oxygen concentrator.

Cindy breathes a "nineteen" as I roll the concentrator under the curtain with my foot and use my teeth to tear the plastic wrapper containing the oxygen tubing. Connecting the clear tube to the Ambu bag, I quickly flip the switch on the oxygen machine, the loud, shrill b-*e-e-e-p* sounding as it kicks on. Meg rushes into the room and to the bedside as I'm turning the oxygen dial up to maximum delivery.

"Call 9-1-1," I quickly instruct her.. "Look in her chart if they ask any questions, but first, tell them she's not breathing, and CPR has been started. Then, find Beth and ask her to call Donna."

Donna is Mrs. White's daughter. She visits every day, entering the nurses' station and making herself at home. On Saturdays, she comes dragging a hamper for her mother's laundry and cradling a chocolate eclair for us nursing staff. I feel a twinge of sadness for her as I think about the wake-up call she's about to receive.

Meg flees the room, her tennis shoes squeaking on the slick, tiled floor.

I take my stethoscope from around my neck and place the bell over Mrs. White's heart. Nothing.

I steal a glance at my watch. "It's been nine minutes."

It feels much longer.

"Need a break?" I ask Cindy, who looks as if she could benefit from some supplemental oxygen herself. She nods as she takes the Ambu bag from my hands.

It feels as if I'm pressing onto a cloth bag of pretzels as the rib bones crack beneath my hands.

After another brutal round of chest compressions I've made in an attempt to restart Mrs. White's 86-year-old heart, Cindy gives two squeezes of the Ambu bag. I place the stethoscope bell over her heart once more.

At first, I think my ears must be deceiving me. I continue to hold the stethoscope very still as I listen intently. Sure enough, the *ba-bum, ba-bum* sound of a beating heart is faintly heard; I'm certain of it.

"Heart sounds!" I nearly exclaim, looking up at Cindy.

She wipes her brow with the back of one hand as I take over the Ambu bag, holding the mask in place over Mrs. White's mouth and nose.

"Grab an IV," I say, nodding my head toward the crash cart at the foot of the bed.

Cindy rifles through the drawers of the large toolbox before producing a syringe full of saline and a package containing an IV cannula. She rushes back to Mrs. White's side and picks up her right arm. She quickly ties on a blue, elastic tourniquet.

At last, we hear the siren, the whirring sound growing closer until it ceases as the ambulance pulls up the hill toward the brick building. The red light flashes through the window, illuminating picture frames and trinkets with each flicker.

EMS personnel enter the room, pushing the long, yellow gurney. One of them asks a question I don't quite catch, but I answer as if I did.

"CPR for fourteen minutes. S1S2 noted at 0743. IV started in the right AC with ten ML's of saline successfully pushed," I inform them.

I take a step back and allow the paramedic to take over. He and his partner each grab ahold of the blankets Mrs. White is lying on.

"Heave-ho, here we go," he chants as he and his partner hoist Mrs. White onto their gurney, the syringe taped to her right arm flapping.

"What's her name?" asks the heavy, mustached paramedic.

"Mable White," I answer.

"Mrs. Mable?" he says loudly into her ear.

"Give my hand a squeeze if you can hear me, Mable."

He and his young, slim "Doogie Howser"-like partner continue working with Mrs. White as they raise the gurney and flee the room.

Cindy and I follow them down the long hallway with residents peering out each doorway.

"....rescue squad!" I hear someone whisper to their roommate.

We quickly approach the intersection where the nurses' station is located. Cindy follows the paramedics and Mrs. White toward the front door as I break off into the small room.

"Tell the ER staff I'll fax over her info," I call over my shoulder. I hastily begin gathering forms to fill out as Beth bounds into the room.

"What else do you need?" she asks. "I called her daughter. She's on her way to meet the ambulance at the hospital."

"Thanks," I reply. "I'm just going to fax over the paperwork. How did Donna sound?"

"Well, she was torn up," Beth says with a sorrowful look. "I felt sorry for her."

"Yeah, I figured so," I say as I turn the front page of Mrs. White's thick chart.

Donna is one of the family members who has allowed their emotions to make important decisions regarding their parents' end-of-life care. According to the documents in my hands, Mrs. White has had an official diagnosis of dementia for ten years. Donna is named the Healthcare Power of Attorney, and she has decided that the best thing for her mother is to receive the utmost scope of treatment for any incident, ailment, or occurrence that falls upon her mother, *including* dying peacefully in her sleep.

Donna means well, and she isn't alone in her wayward mindset. That is made evident when I scan the rows of patient charts against the wall and note small neon yellow stickers that indicate the "full code" status. It is disheartening to realize that because of this, many of my patients are robbed of the ability to approach death with dignity.

I'll fall asleep tonight with visions of Mrs. White's small, frail body trying to pass away from this world while I, bound by law, try ferociously and violently to stop it. I personally find it absurdly barbaric.

"Bless her heart," Beth says, interrupting my thoughts on ethics.

I look up to see her slowly shaking her head, a look of empathy on her mature face.

Beth has been a nurse for longer than I've been alive, and she isn't afraid to voice her disapproval of the evolution of healthcare "practices, procedures, and policies."

We share an unspoken agreement that what Cindy and I just did in room 113 was nearly heinous, but we follow policy (loosely, for the most part) and continue our duties.

"I know," I agree. "She's going to be so lost without her mom."

"Well!" Beth snaps as she takes her reading glasses from the top of her head and places them on the bridge of her nose.

"Can I do anything else for you?"

"Oh no, I'm fine. I'll just go finish passing out the meds. You go finish too," I urge with a wave.

Beth, Cindy, and I will likely be behind for the rest of the day.

My legs still feel like Jell-O as I attempt to pick up where I left off. The adrenaline from this morning's chaos has left me feeling fatigued and moving at the speed of a slug. Thankfully, Meg has taken charge of things, and she's met the residents' needs as best she can. On top of my medicine cart, I find a small list in Meg's handwriting:

Mrs. Edwards wants pain pill

Claude needs enema

Mary O. puked at 8 AM

Such a lovely little note. I can't help but giggle a little as I push it aside. I'll go ahead and skip to Mrs. Edwards so that I can administer her pain pill along with all her other medications. I'll delegate the enema administration to Meg, and ask her to keep an eye on Mary O.

All of the residents are having breakfast, including the diabetic residents who are currently in the dining room. I'm neither allowed to pull them away from their meal or administer any type of mediation at the table, and because there are many administrative staff members buzzing around at this hour, I have no choice but to wait until after breakfast. I'll then take each of my seven insulin-dependent diabetic patients to their rooms where I will administer their shots. Then, I'll call the house doctor and list each resident's name, telling him of the medication errors that took place on my watch. While I'm at it, I'll let him know that Mrs. White went into cardiac arrest this morning and left the facility via ambulance at 0750.

"Hey, good lookin," my husband's familiar voice interrupts my diligence.

I look up from my mountain of paperwork and turn to see Joseph standing behind me in his police uniform, holding a plastic grocery bag.

"Oh, hey!" I greet him, surprised. "What'cha got?"

"I thought you'd need a little something, and someone to see that you ate it," he explains, extending the bag toward me.

Then he continues, "I heard on the radio. I knew you'd be needing *something*."

I lay the handful of papers on the table.

"What on Earth did I do to deserve you?" I ask as I reach for the bag in his hand. "What did you bring me? I *do* feel like I might perish. I didn't even have time to eat my lunch."

"I just went by the grocery store and picked up some of your favorites," he replies.

In the bag are pistachio nuts, fruit jerky, grass-fed beef sticks, and –

I gasp as I hold up the bag of dark chocolate peanut butter cups.

"Yes!" I exclaim. "You're really the best. And I love you."

Joseph gives a satisfied grin. "You're welcome," he says.

"What has this sweet man gone and done now?" I hear Cindy ask as she enters the room.

"Oh, he brought me some snacks. He sure knows the way to my heart – as if he doesn't already have that," I add with a wink.

"Well aren't you a sweetheart?" Cindy coos at Joseph with a giggle.

He looks at me and blushes beet red.

"I'll see you this evening," he says as he takes me into a quick embrace.

"I hope I'm not very late," I reply.

I glance at my watch to see that it's just after three o'clock. I will need to get things wrapped up and begin the supper-time medication round in less than an hour. I deeply hope no catastrophes strike between now and then.

"He *is* the sweetest, isn't he?" I say to Cindy as the heavy door latches behind Joseph.

"He's just darling!" she exclaims. "What did he bring you, anyway?" Cindy asks as she rifles through the bag on the table.

"Organic pistachios, organic fruit jerky, organic grass-fed beef sticks, organic candy, that kombucha stuff you drink. My goodness, I bet'cha I could've bought a tank of gas for what this little bag cost!" Cindy laughs as she helps herself to a piece of dried pineapple.

"Don't mind if I do," she says with a grin.

"I know it *is* kind of a rip-off, how they charge so much more for that "organic" label," I say. "But at least I know they had to adhere to *some* standards and the fruits and nuts aren't as likely to have been sprayed with poisonous pesticides."

"Hmm. It sounds like I've interrupted a great conversation." The words come from an unfamiliar voice behind me. I turn around to see a young woman standing in the doorway of the nurses' station, wearing a broad smile and holding a fat baby on her hip.

I laugh, a bit taken aback and also a bit captivated by her boldness. Her long, wavy hair is the color of a penny, and she wears a long, pink floral dress with a pleated peplum. The picture of old-fashioned beauty.

She senses mine and Cindy's loss for words and introduces herself.

"I'm sorry; my name is Violet. We were here visiting our friend - Ms. Maude Cochran in room 206, and she asked me to come and find her nurse to see if she could have a pain pill," the woman explains.

"I don't mean to bother you." Violet half-winces.

"I think that knee is really bothering her, though. Just when you get a chance!"

"I'll bring it right down," Cindy answers, walking swiftly out the door of the nurses' station.

As she fumbles in her pocket for her keys to the medicine cart, I admire Violet's happy baby girl with her chunky legs kicking in delight.

"She's so precious," I comment as I rub her little foot.

"Thank you," Violet says. "This is Esther." She coos as if she's talking to the baby instead.

"Well, Miss Esther is just beautiful. Look at those dark curls! Her dad must be dark headed; it's such a contrast to your red," I say, mesmerized by the both of them.

"Yes, he is," Violet answers proudly. "Half of our children have red hair like me, and the other half have his dark hair."

"That's so special. How many do you have?" I ask.

"Six, and counting," she replies with a smile as she kisses the top of baby Esther's curly black hair. "They're all down in Ms. Maude's room right now." She smiles as she points toward the 200-wing.

Against my better judgment, I quickly abandon all my tasks at hand and exit the nurses' station with Violet.

"I can take it to her," I say as I approach Cindy's medicine cart.

She grins as she passes me the small plastic cup containing the round white pill, before pushing her reading glasses back onto the top of her head.

"Thanks," she mumbles with the slice of dehydrated pineapple between her teeth.

"I overheard what you were saying about the chemicals on our food," Violet says as we walk down the tiled hallway. "I feel the same way, and it's nice to hear someone else express those beliefs."

"I wasn't always so aware," I admit. "Not until a couple of years ago. Now, I'm the black sheep everywhere I go." I laugh, but it's no joke.

"I totally get that," Violet says. "And if you continue on that path, you'll meet resistance regularly. But, let it be a propeller that pushes you forward, and never let it discourage you from doing what you feel in your gut."

"That's good advice," I reply. "I definitely get my share of ridicule. Mostly it doesn't bother me."

"I think most people genuinely don't understand. Sad as it is, being aware of what you consume is a foreign concept in today's culture."

"That's definitely true," I reply as we approach Ms. Maude's doorway.

"Knock, knock," I call as we enter the room.

"I hear you need something for pain, Ms. Maude. Cindy sent this by me," I explain.

"Okay," Ms. Maude says as she takes the medicine from me. "This knee is giving me a fit today." She swallows the pill down with a sip of water before chunking the empty cup into the trash can by her chair.

"Thank you, honey," she says. "Now, I want you to look at all these children I've got visiting me." Ms. Maude beams with the gladness that seems to be taking the edge off her knee pain.

I glance around the room at the children, some lying across the small bed and some occupying the window seat. They appear to range in age from around three to eleven years old, if I had to guess. Just as Violet described, three of them have bright copper hair, and the other two have jet black hair like Esther.

"Hi!" I greet them as their wandering eyes look up at me. I can't fathom the burst of happiness brought by the sight of the roomful of bright-eyed children I've just met.

"They're beautiful," I assure Violet as I look at her with delight and a pinch of envy.

"Thank you," she replies with a definite twinkle of gratitude in her eyes.

"Well, I guess I'd better be going." I look at Ms. Maude who is smiling from her recliner by the bed.

"What's your hurry?" she asks, genuinely.

"If I told you, you wouldn't believe me," I answer.

"Well, find a spot to sit down and tell us, anyway," Ms. Maude says with a chuckle.

Knowing I don't have time, I found myself sitting on the foot of the bed. I didn't tell of my workday troubles, but I know I wasn't really expected to anyway. Instead, we talked of farming in the 1930's, raising a family, and canning green beans.

With one of Violet's energetic little boys wiggling on my lap, I expressed my desire to learn how to preserve food myself. That's one thing I never picked up from Grandmama. I guess I was too young to learn back when she was still able to do it.

"I have an extra canner I'd be glad to give you, if you want to learn," Violet had said. "It still has the little booklet with recipes in it and everything!"

"Sure, I would," I excitedly agreed.

Despite my offer to come get it myself, or meet Violet here at work, she insisted that she'd deliver it to my house.

"Are you sure?" I asked. "I don't want you to have to drag all the kids out, just for me."

"They won't mind, I promise. Just look at Benjamin," she said, pointing to the red-headed toddler balancing on my knees.

I smiled and nodded in agreement before giving her my address. She promised to bring the canning pot over tomorrow morning, along with some recipes.

I finally said goodbye to them all and reluctantly went back to finish my work, fully aware that I was even further behind than I'd been before and probably wouldn't be able to leave until well after dark.

Yet, I felt an odd sense of warm uncertainty as I returned to the nurses' station. I hadn't had a pleasant conversation with a woman near my own age since Jill moved away, and it seemed such a fateful surprise.

At 7:15 PM, I'm still not finished with the day's work. I pull my cardigan from my bag and push my arms into the soft sleeves as I complete the last of the paperwork in the dim, dusty nurses' station. I've passed along the responsibility to the night shift nurse already, so all I need to do is finish this morning's incident report in detail. I strain my exhausted mind to remember the exact timeline of events.

There was no time to write anything down during the chaotic event, so I will have to allow my memory to serve me the best I can as I write the notes. As I recall each detail of what could have been a simple, peaceful death, I wonder how Donna is doing. I had imagined she'd be over by now, tearfully recounting the day as it happened from her point of view as she sifted through her mother's belongings to find that special outfit.

"Close enough," I whisper to myself as I close Mrs. White's chart, satisfied that my notes are thorough and lawsuit-proof, should Donna make an irrational, emotional decision to investigate the facility in hopes of assuaging the sting of her sudden loss. Though not likely, it's always possible.

My tired body sinks into the car seat as I drive home. The drive feels longer than normal; I can't wait to get into a warm bath and forget about the day. Thankfully, I don't have to work tomorrow. The fine perks of working twelve-hour shifts are the days off in between.

"You made it. Finally," Joseph says as I enter the front door, dragging my feet.

"What is it about a code that wipes me completely out for the rest of the day?" I ask with a chuckle as I drop my large bag onto the floor. Dill rushes to greet me.

"Those mental images are a lot," he answers. And he's right. The physical labor of performing CPR is tough for even the fittest, but the emotional burden is heavier. Joseph knows this firsthand.

"I'm just so happy to be home," I say as I head over to the kitchen and pour myself a large glass of water.

Joseph follows me and leans against the cabinets as I gulp down every drop.

"I see you're in your PJs already," I comment breathlessly. "What'd you have for supper?"

"Don't scold," he snickers with a side-eyed glare. "I grabbed a pizza. I saved you some, if you want it," he adds.

"I'm okay. I think I'll have some yogurt with that granola I made, after my bath. Then, I'm crashing."

"I don't blame you," Joseph replies as he stretches and yawns. "I'm pretty worn out myself."

"Oh, I almost forgot! Today did have a silver lining."

"Tell me," he says, still leaned against the cabinets.

"Well, I met this girl. Well — woman. And she seems pretty amazing." I say it as if it's a question.

"Oh, really?" Joseph stifles a laugh.

"Yes, really. She came in to visit one of the acute care patients. She has lots of cute kids, and she is *so* sweet. And she's going to bring me one of those pressure canners tomorrow and she said she'd teach me how to *can* things! Grandmama used to can sometimes, but she just made jams and pickles, and anyway, I never learned."

I pause for a breath. I'm suddenly giddy with excitement as I tell Joseph about Violet, my possible newfound friend.

"That'll be good for you. You need a new girlfriend since Jill's gone," he comments.

"Yeah. She seems so wise. *Beautiful* too. She has fiery red hair down to here..." I show him with my hand in the small of my back.

"And three of her children have hair the same color," I almost exclaim.

Joseph snickers. "Yeah?" he asks, folding his arms.

"Oh, don't make fun of me," I playfully chide.

"I seem to have gotten a second wind, now," I declare as I pace briskly across the living room, Joseph following behind. From the bench by the foot of the staircase, I pick up Addie's soft, leather-bound diary.

"I'm going to soak in the tub for a while." I give Joseph a peck on his stubbly cheek before sprinting up the oak staircase.

FOUR

I haven't written in a while. For no other reason than I haven't felt the desire to. Some days, the loneliness pierces like a dart. Without warning, its pang nearly sends me to my knees in desolation. Most days, I can stay busy enough to keep the pangs at bay; but then there are those rare occasions where I have no prenatal appointments scheduled, no expectant or postpartum mothers are in need, Madge is out of town, and even the petunias don't seem to thirst for water.

It's in these idle days that I find myself thinking of what could've been. I should be traveling through the late-fall season of life with Isaiah by my side. He should be sitting next to me on the porch rocker at this very minute, listening to the wild sounds of summer. We should have grandchildren running barefooted about the farm, catching butterflies and digging for earthworms. Our son should be here, enjoying an abundant life.

I should come in from an all-night birthing to Isaiah standing in the kitchen wearing his denim overalls, making coffee for himself and me. I'd saunter over to him, my shoulders laden with weariness, and accept a steamy black cup that I'd only sip before secretly pouring it down the drain after he'd gone out to do the chores. Then, I'd steep a small but strong cup of chamomile tea and take it to my rose oil bath with me before retiring to the bed for a restful nap.

In these quiet, still moments, the sadness can swallow me up if I allow it. And I almost did, this morning. I sat on the front porch before daybreak and held my tea until it went cold. I stared out across the foggy field through the faintest hint of light. The pasture fence Isaiah put up all those years ago is still holding strong, housing Ginger and her baby, and the laying hens.

I sat for a long while in the quiet of the early morning, feeling rather sorry for myself. That's really what it boils down to - feeling sorry for myself - and it's very easy to do at times. However unhealthy it may be, I cannot allow myself to succumb to tears of anguish because I fear that if I did, they'd never cease. But finally, as always, I stood up and shook the grief from my shoulders, sending it away for another day. I decided I'd go into town and do a bit of shopping.

The old Mercedes seemed to know the way as we meandered slowly toward town. Through the thousands of towering pines the country roads are etched into. Down the long stretch of highway, away from the mountains and into the peach sunrise. And over the railroad tracks as I entered the little town of Weatherford.

White houses with large porches and vibrant hydrangeas were evenly spaced. The sidewalk in front of them was shaded by weeping willows and mimosa trees until suddenly the houses were replaced with the bustling shoppes of town.

Downtown was just beginning to awaken as I crept down the shady street. Retirees and young mothers with children walked along the cobblestone sidewalk beneath the towering elms and flowering crepe myrtles.

I parked somewhere near the middle of town and sauntered slowly down the beautiful, uneven walkway myself. The aroma coming from the town bakery hung in the morning air, inviting me to step inside.

I ordered a cinnamon scone and a cup of coffee with cream, taking time to enjoy the pastry from a small table by the window. There, I nibbled slowly and watched as people passed by, taking notice of their facial expressions and body language. I found that most of them appeared happy, some rushed, still a few somber. Like myself.

Then, bringing my coffee, I slowly continued down the stone walk until I reached my most frequented bay window shoppe in town: Hammond's Natural Market. There, I filled my basket with staples I needed a replenishment of - lavender oil, Belladonna pearls, dried chamomile flowers (since my plants cannot keep up with my needs.) Then some things I needed for birthing and expectant mothers - raspberry leaf and oat straw, jasmine and copaiba oils, dried dandelion root.

I had a forced but friendly conversation with the owner, Ms. Hammond as I made my purchase, and then I left the store to continue my stroll. Gray clouds moved in and hid the sunlight for the remainder of my day out, a direct reflection of my inward emotions.

I thought of Madge as I window-shopped Weatherford. I wondered what she might be up to and imagined her walking barefooted along the beach this morning as she scanned the shore for soft blue sea glass. I'll ask her to join me for a day on the town once she returns from her trip. She had asked me to come along to her beach cottage, as she does nearly every time she takes a trip down to the Carolina coast. But as usual, I reminded her that I couldn't leave the farm or the mothers and babies. "One day soon," I promised her.

Walking along with only my thoughts and an armful of merchandise in a brown paper bag reminded me of a very special piece of my childhood. Some of my most precious memories which are carved out and set in the center of my mind forever, are the ones of my very young years. No matter where I go in the world, those memories shall be there, waiting to beckon me back in a time such as this.

Through my loneliness and even anguish at times, I know that a part of me lives back in that quaint country cottage in the lush green valley, surrounded by family, friends, and firelight. Sheep graze the hills beyond the wisteria-adorned cottage. Geese squawk and tuttle about the farmyard. Mother pours me a cup of fresh milk with cinnamon, and smiles as she gracefully touches the tip of my nose. I'd give anything to go back there; but I know that the memories nestled within my soul comfort my ache and propel me forward when I need it most.

I looked down at my left hand as I strolled along, studying the claddagh ring that Mother gave to me when I was only six years old. What once fit my index finger, I've only worn on my smallest one for many years, and I've no plans of ever removing it.

I studied the perfectly detailed golden hands holding a genuine emerald heart in the center; the crown above the heart having just as much tiny detail as the little hands. I was reminded again of how proud I was that Mother trusted me with her treasured ring. As I grew older, the pride also grew as I realized she treasured me more than she treasured the ring. I wonder what she'd say if she knew little Adelaide would still be wearing it when her hands were wrinkled with the passage of many years.

I took my time about, sauntering through the warm, southern town. Up one side of the shady street, down the other. I returned to my car and drove further away from home, to a frequented consignment shoppe where I perused every nook and cranny. I had the pleasure of finding a second-hand pottery mug, a powder-blue shawl, and a handful of books.

Though normally out of character for me, I had lunch out and I didn't feel one bit guilty for it. I stopped at a small sandwich shoppe, where I sat down and indulged in a toasted reuben with homemade chips fried in who-knows-what. It was a satisfying meal nonetheless.

Once I'd had enough of the town, I made one last stop at Tilia's Coffee Shop for a cup of peppermint tea, where I paced the small, dimly-lit café while I waited for my tea to steep. Then I set out for home, taking the long way back to Bascomb.

As I drove through the country, I was reminded quite a few times of the age-old saying that goes something like, "Just because we <u>can </u>doesn't mean we <u>should</u>."

First, I drove past what would have been a beautiful scene to most others. The apple orchard spread as far as the eye could see up the hillside, but what I sadly noticed was the dead grass beneath each tree that told me they'd all been sprayed with poison.

Sure, it's perfectly sensible for the apple farmer to produce fruit for his consumers that aren't half-eaten by pests. That wouldn't be very profitable. However, it comes at a very high cost for the consumer, to be able to enjoy a crisp, beautiful apple, free from bugs or holes.

The next atrocity was smelled miles before it was seen. Out in the once-open field were the long, rectangular confinement houses for the grocery store chickens. Whoever owns the operation couldn't care less about the health of the forty thousand birds that are crammed into each of the buildings without sunlight, or a natural diet, or even the ability to open their wings or to stretch their legs. It doesn't matter to them if the birds get sick from inhaling fecal matter twenty-four-seven or if the consumers get sick from the medications given to the birds, or the disinfecting solution the meat is dipped into. Money matters more. On second thought, perhaps money is the only thing that matters.

I tried to enjoy my trip back to Bascomb, but the troubling thoughts swirling about my mind were a bit distracting. I began to think of the many unnecessary interventions and inventions that so often cause more harm than good in today's world. Health and well-being swapped for conveniences, mostly in the name of the almighty dollar, the consumers none the wiser.

We can take away folks' critical thinking capabilities and imaginations by replacing thought-provoking problems with computers that do the 'thinking' for them. We can make it so that people are able to complete tasks with one touch of a finger and not so much as a droplet of sweat upon their brow.

We can add artificial colorants and flavors to already-red, already-sweet fruits. Insult the Creator of the land by molesting His masterpiece with fertilizers, machinery, and lack of regard for its pure and perfect existence.

We can. But, just because we <u>can</u>, does not mean we <u>should</u>.

As for the things that I do have control over, I'm getting along fine. Ginger and I had an unspoken therapy session as I stood in the barn and brushed her slick coat this evening. She's still a proud mama, ever loving to her young bull calf.

Next, I checked on the bees, who were working hard, dancing all about the anise hyssop, borage, and lavender that I've planted in abundance just for them. Their rich, dark honey will be delectable this fall in a steamy cup of tea.

I then picked the garden, put the chickens to bed, and took a stroll to the edge of the field. The wild blackberries hung onto the thorny bushes in perfectly plump abundance. I harvested as much as I felt like harvesting, piling the dark, juicy berries on top of the tomatoes and cucumbers in my basket.

My teacup is empty, and my hand is growing tired. I'm uncertain if I will retire to bed early, or stay up a bit and work on my puzzle. It's an autumn scene, covered with difficult but beautiful auburn leaves. My heart longs for the crisp fall days that promise a bit of rest and perhaps some comfort from whatever ails the spirit. However, each season brings purpose and beauty of its own, and I do relish that profound realization.

I hope to hear from Madge tomorrow. I expect her back in a few days, and I anticipate our reunion with gladness. Maybe one of my mothers will call on me for some advice of some sort. Hopefully nothing too serious; no one is due just yet. I am hopeful that morning brings me lightened spirits and cloudless skies.

Until next time

Addie

FIVE

The first thing I think of as I face the morning sun is Addie. Many days, she awoke from her bed in perhaps this very same room and could hardly muster the strength to face the day. I feel the slightest twinge of guilt for being happy here. But I know Addie well enough to know that she'd rebuke that notion as quick as a wink.

I also think of how much I can relate to her as she reminisces on the joyous days of her childhood. My own will be carried with me for as long as I live.

"Morning," I mutter sleepily as I sit up in bed and stretch my arms above my head.

"Morning, beautiful," Joseph replies. He stands with his back to the large window, blocking the sun from my tender eyes as he fastens the buttons on his uniform shirt.

"I'll start your coffee." I clumsily swing my feet onto the floor and pull my plush robe on before slowly padding down the stairs toward the bright kitchen. I can't help but feel bubbly with excitement, even as my aching body begs for more sleep.

When I gave Violet my address, she said she'd be here at ten this morning; I have plenty of time to lay back down, but I think I'll have an espresso and start cleaning in preparation for her welcomed arrival.

I miss Jill so very much. I value our long-distance friendship immensely, but meeting Violet struck something in me. I'm just not so sure what.

The morning sun pours into the kitchen as I stir around, making coffees and packing Joseph's lunch. Today, he'll get homemade chicken salad on sourdough bread, and his coworkers will tease him, as usual. He tells me it's a running joke between them all that "Blaire won't let him eat junk food." Which isn't true; I just refuse to bring *food-like products* into our home or put them into his lunchbox.

"Thanks, babe," Joseph says, taking the warm ceramic cup from my hand.

I wink as I watch him take the first sip through a cloud of steam.

"Call me later, if you have time. I hope you have fun with–what's her name? Vera?"

"*Violet*," I correct him with a snicker.

"Oh, yeah. *Violet,* " he replies as he takes his large lunch bag off the kitchen table.

With a squeeze around the waist and a peck on the cheek, he's off to fight the crimes in Bascomb for the next eight hours.

Dill is still upstairs snoring like a bear from the middle of our queen-sized bed. Any other morning, I would quickly lock the door and scurry back up to the bed to curl up to his soft, warm body that radiates heat like a furnace. But this morning, I'm too excited for sleep.

As I stand munching on my buttered toast and sipping my frothy espresso from Daddy's old Rise & Shine Hardee's mug, I scan the kitchen and living room. I need to fold the quilt and spread it over the couch, straighten the books on the coffee table, wash up the dishes, get dressed...

What should I wear? Should I wear makeup or embrace the natural look? I could put on some fun instrumental music in the background. No, it would be too much with the sounds of the children playing. Surely Violet plans to bring the children, right? I probably shouldn't light any candles in case one of them gets burned.

I wonder if she likes coffee, or tea? I could have something hot and ready when she arrives. But maybe she likes neither. I guess I'll just have to ask her when she gets here.

I'm not sure if anyone will be going upstairs or not, but on my way up to change clothes, I wipe down the slick, oak banister and scrub the toilet just in case.

Then, I shuffle into the bedroom and make the bed before choosing an outfit. Standing in front of the wardrobe mirror, I hold first one dress in front of me, and then the other. Should I go with the pale blue, or the burgundy? Maybe I should forget the dresses altogether and wear jeans and a sweatshirt.

"What are you doing?" I ask myself. "Does it even matter? Violet doesn't care what you wear."

Suddenly I have a sinking thought. One that I hadn't even considered before. What if Violet simply drops off the pressure cooker on the porch and then *leaves*? That's possible, considering we didn't discuss any plans. I didn't actually invite her over, after all, so she may feel uncomfortable coming inside. She probably won't even want to get all the kids out of the car.

Racing back downstairs wearing a pair of jeans and a cotton tee-shirt, I realize the uncertainties will soon be put to rest as I hear the crunch of a car driving across the gravel driveway. Dill hears it, too. He runs to the door, his tail fanning back and forth as he stands on his hind legs and peers out the dirty, nose-smudged window. Dang it, I should've cleaned that.

Following close behind him, I look out as well. Violet steps out of a white minivan and walks to the back of it as the children begin to climb out.

"Yes! They're all getting out, Dill!" I exclaim. He looks up at me from beneath furrowed brows.

I count one, two, three, four children as they pile out of the vehicle and gather around their mother. She must've left the other two with her husband.

As Violet closes the rear door of her van with the large silver pot under her arm, I notice a strange look on her face as she gazes around the yard and up the height of the house.

Amusement? No, not quite…more like *bewildered* amusement.

I open the storm door and walk out onto the porch to greet the family as they cross the front yard.

"Hey!" I call as I wave to them from the front steps. The kids run and skip their way toward the house, all gleefully present. Violet, however, saunters slowly as she approaches the house, her green dress swaying in the breeze.

Smiling, she studies her surroundings. First at the barn, then the herb beds left by Addie. She continues to take in every sight with a look of amazement on her face. It's almost as if she's never seen a genuine old farmhouse before. As if she's in awe of her wonderful surroundings.

Finally, she speaks as she approaches the front steps and joins me and her children who are all chattering happily.

"I knew the address sounded familiar," Violet says. Though she's merry, her facial expression holds more of a sentimental one.

"Oh?" I ask, perplexed.

Violet steps up onto the porch as I relieve her of the large, bulky pot. Sitting it on a nearby table, I continue trying to read her unspoken explanation for being familiar with my home. As I look expectantly at her, she simply shakes her head as if in awe.

Finally, she begins to explain as she stands next to me, looking out across the front yard. "Did you know the woman who lived here before you?" she asks.

"Addie?" I ask, surprised.

"Yes!" Violet breathes. She seems pleased, and a bit relieved by my answer.

"Well," I begin. "That's a long story. Why don't we have a seat?"

Violet and I sit on the wooden porch swing together as the kids run squealing around the yard, playing with Dill. My heart races as I attempt to calmly tell the story of how Addie became a part of my life, though I'm dying to know the same about Violet; I can't believe I'm talking to someone else who knew Addie. I surely never thought it would come to be.

"I knew Addie. Yet, I didn't *know* that I knew her," I begin.

"That doesn't make any sense at all, does it?" I stifle a laugh.

Violet smiles expectantly as I continue.

"I found this house a couple of years ago, right after it went on the market, and I knew I just had to have it. It reminded me so much of my childhood home and, well…at *that* time, my career and memories from my childhood were the only positive things in my whole life. And the former was questionable some days."

"Well, right before I moved in, not only did I meet my husband, but I also found a nightstand at an antique store which happened to have a diary inside the drawer. I began reading it and was absolutely *enthralled* by Addie's words. I sought her out, but had no luck. I had no idea who she was or where she was from. So, I just continued reading the thoughts she'd written down, and they became such a comfort to me. I connected with Addie in that we were both lonely and pretty much only had our work, helping other people, to keep us busy. She really inspired me to see the beauty in life, and to push through the pain of grief, ya know?"

I pause as Violet listens intently, hanging onto every word. She quickly glances toward the kids then smiles knowingly and nods, waiting for me to continue.

"So, I came to a part in the diary where she talked about the rehab after her knee replacement. Lo and behold, she was at *Sunny Meadows,* and she named *me* in her diary. I was flabbergasted when I realized that "Addie" was actually Ms. Adelaide, who I'd cared for but didn't truly see until much too late. I could kick myself now..." I almost trail off, but quickly snap back.

"Anyway, I did some digging in the old medical records at work, and I found out that her address was...here. I was *floored,* let me tell you."

I snicker softly as I remember that night on the musty closet's floor, sleep deprived, horrified, and blown away by the shocking revelations.

"Wow!" Violet says, eyes wide. "That is quite the story!"

"I know," I agree. "It really still blows me away to think about it. I mean, what are the odds?"

"Well… do you know anything else about her?" Violet asks. "I mean, did she write anything interesting in the diary?"

"Oh, the best birth stories I've ever heard, advice I never asked for but am happy to heed…and a special – albeit *peculiar* friendship. See, the first diary isn't the only one. Upstairs, underneath the closet floorboards, was a stack of them. I've really gotten to know who Addie was, but I'm sort of sad because I'm nearing the end of her diaries… I have fully indulged in her words, I guess you could say."

"Tell me, Blaire…Did she ever write anything about a woman named Madge?" Violet finally asks, wearing a cunning smile.

"Oh, yes," I reply. "That was her truest friend. She mentions her a lot in her diaries. Why?" I ask, intrigued.

"Well…Madge is my mom," Violet replies.

As she says this, a rush seems to blow over me, leaving raised chill bumps on my arms. I remember feeling much the same sensation many times during the course of the revelations of who Addie was.

"No way," is all I can utter before covering my mouth.

"I'm just as stunned as you are, believe me," Violet says. "When I pulled up, I was flooded with memories of Addie. Being here feels so strange. I was here with Mom countless times while I was growing up."

Violet's soft smile fades into a somber expression as she reflects on the days of her past. I wonder if they're happy memories.

I remember trying to get in touch with Madge a couple of times following the discoveries I'd made about Addie. I'd found her phone number in the old files as Addie's "responsible party", but I never had any luck contacting her.

I'm afraid to ask, but gently I do.

"Is your mom still with us?"

Violet slowly shakes her head as she looks up from her lap. "Not long after Addie passed, Mom had an accident. She broke her hip so severely that she never got out of bed after the surgery. And she just…gave up her spirit." Violet wipes a tear from her cheek.

"Oh, no. I'm so sorry," I whisper.

Violet is quiet for a moment as she looks out toward the old barn. Finally, she laughs between sniffles.

"One time, I had come with Mom to visit Addie, and when we got here–" she points toward the driveway where her van is parked. "Addie was running as fast as she could with a rooster chasing her. He was hot on her heels…" Violet bursts into laughter as tears roll down both cheeks, all of her emotions seeming to come together in one joyful expression.

"It's the only time I can recall ever seeing Addie run. She was so graceful most of the time, you know." Violet gains her composure as she dabs at her eyes with the sleeve of her cardigan.

I laugh at both the mental image of Addie being chased by a rooster, and Violet's recollection of the memorable event.

"Well, I haven't read about that in any of her diaries. But I can see it happening as you describe it."

"I'm also glad you said that about her grace and poise, because it's exactly how I picture her to be. I only ever saw her in person during her short stay at The Home – that's what I call it – and I don't think she was very much herself then."

"No, she probably wasn't. Addie was very independent. I guess she had to be after Isaiah died," Violet says.

"Well, do you want to round up the kids and go inside where it's warmer? I've got a fire burning."

Today isn't as frigid as it has been lately, but it's still a bit chilly.

"Sure." Violet smiles as she stands from the swing.

"Come on kids, let's go inside!" She playfully coaxes the four children onto the porch. As they clumsily gather around, I feel a longing pull so heavily it feels as though it bounds me where I stand. Someday, my own children will surely play on this very porch.

Inside, the air is so warm it seems to welcome us all into a big hug. As Violet and the kids pull their shoes off and pile them on the rug by the door, I walk the short distance over to the kitchen with Dill following behind me.

"You don't have to do that!" I say. "But please make yourself comfortable. And my idea of comfort is shoeless, so go right ahead."

I laugh at my own banter, but thankfully so does Violet. "Us, too," she says.

"Would you guys like some chamomile tea?" I ask, holding up a mason jar full of tiny yellow and white flowers.

"Oh, I would, please. How about you guys?" she asks the children.

"Yes, please!" they excitedly chime in unison, the boys jumping up and down.

"I get super excited for tea, too!" I assure them with a smile as I turn and reach for the teapot.

We sit around the living room, each enjoying our honey-sweetened teas by the wood stove, with Dill lying peacefully on the couch and taking up enough space for at least three people.

"I have some games!" I announce as I remember my cabinet full of board games which I've collected over the last year since Joseph and I have been married. Each time I've bought one to add to the collection, I've felt very thankful to have someone to play them with.

"Why don't y'all open that cabinet there beside the bookshelf, and see if there is anything that looks like fun?" I point to the aged wooden cabinet that holds checkers, Monopoly, card games, and dominoes.

The kids happily rush to the cabinet and quarrel over which one they'll play first.

"Well, does the house look anything like it did when Addie lived here?" I ask.

Violet looks up at the top of the door frame that leads to the stairs.

"Well, she always had herbs hanging to dry over the doors and anywhere she could find a space. She had baskets everywhere, too. Like this one…" She briskly walks over to the kitchen counter and picks up my egg basket.

Then she continues. "They held things, they hung from things, sometimes they just sat around waiting to contain all of her garden vegetables or eggs or herbs or her beautiful cut flowers."

"And she always had jars of things lined up on the countertops, or on the windowsills… glass jars of honey with different spices in them, herbs infusing into oils for her homemade salves she liked to make. There were braids of garlic and onions hanging around in the kitchen. Books… books everywhere."

Violet trails off as she glances around the kitchen and living room, taking in the old familiar home.

"Sometimes, when Mom and I would come over, Addie would be buzzing around in the kitchen making things, with the sounds of Celtic music playing on her record player."

"She sure was a special lady," she finally says as she slowly walks back toward the couch and takes a seat.

"She sure was," I agree. "As dramatic as it sounds, I wouldn't be the same person without her."

"But your mom must have been pretty special herself, to be valued so by Addie. She writes so fondly of her good friend, Madge."

"Oh, she was. And they were two peas in a pod. I miss her so much. I miss both of them," Violet says quietly.

"Would you mind if I read some of the things Addie wrote about Mom?"

"Come with me," I say as I stand from the couch and set my teacup on the coffee table.

"Are the kids okay to stay here?" she asks as we head toward the staircase in the hall.

"Oh, sure. They can't hurt anything," I reply, turning on the hall light.

"Kids, I'll be right back. I'm going to go upstairs with Ms. Blaire, alright? Be sure you stay right here."

Upstairs, Violet and I stand in front of the large bookshelf by the window of my bedroom.

"Oh, the memories," she says. "I didn't spend too much time in this room, but it still looks just like it did the last time I was here…probably twenty years ago, now."

I point to the row of diaries, in their special place. Each one has its own pattern on the cover, and each one is worn. I run my finger along the spines before choosing one near the middle of the collection, which has purple irises on the cover.

"I think *this one,* if I'm not mistaken, has a lot of Madge in it," I say as I hand the diary to Violet.

"Oh..." is all she can say as she takes it, her eyes becoming glassy.

"I want you to take it. After all, I have plenty." I snicker awkwardly.

"You have no idea how much this means," Violet says as she holds the floral notebook to her chest.

"I don't know how I could ever repay you for this," she whispers.

"Please, just fill me full of all the stories you can think of," I beg.

"These diaries, this house —and now your memories — are all I have left of Addie."

"She's really influenced your life hasn't she?" Violet asks, wearing an impish grin.

"More than I could put into words," I reply. "As I said before, my life would probably look a lot different if it weren't for me finding that old diary in this old thing..."

I walk across the creaky hardwood floor and run my hand along the nightstand.

"I would have never known to look under the floorboards for the rest of the diaries. I wouldn't have learned about herbal remedies or to appreciate the beauty in the simple things in life, like birds singing…fresh bread…the miracle of birth. Speaking of which, did Addie deliver any of your babies?"

"My three oldest. She even delivered *me*. Of course, I don't remember much about that," Violet says with a chuckle.

She grows quiet for several seconds before she continues. "Addie was wonderful at my babies' births. Sarah gave me the hardest time…she couldn't get fixed exactly right in the birth canal. So, Addie lovingly maneuvered me when I couldn't any longer, rolling me from side to side in between the contractions. Mom was there too, rubbing my back and placing cold washcloths on my forehead. And finally, I felt her slip down. She was born quickly after that into Addie's hands. That labor lasted about eight hours."

Violet leans against the bookcase as she continues to recount the births of her children.

"Then, Grace was born quickly and gracefully – her name was fitting," she adds.

"I remember Addie asking me if I wanted to feel her hair as she was crowning and I shouted an emphatic 'No!' through the pushes." Violet and I both laugh.

"I apologized later for shouting at her, to which she scolded me for apologizing."

"Anyway, less than a minute later, Grace was born, with a headful of black hair and a nice set of lungs. Addie handed her to me at once and I held and admired her for hours and hours…Then when Paul came along, Addie *almost* missed the birth altogether!"

"Really?" I ask, intrigued.

"Yes, he came so quickly. Actually, all of them have besides Sarah. But by now, I've gotten comfortable enough that I don't mind too much if the midwife doesn't make it. I have one that I use – her name is Carol – but my husband caught our youngest because Carol was an hour away at the *apple festival* when I called her." Violet giggles at the memory.

"Your husband doesn't freak out or anything?" I ask.

"John? No way," she assures me with a wave of her hand.

"He's gotten so used to birth by now, it doesn't bother him at all. I think he was secretly glad when Carol didn't make it, if you want my honest opinion." Violet snickers again before walking through the bedroom door and leaning over the banister to peek at the children.

"I've really enjoyed reading all the birth stories in Addie's diaries. And I have truly learned so much about birth that I never even considered before. Things that contradict what I've learned in school and have even applied at my job."

Butterflies tickle my stomach at the thought of having children, as Violet and I meander back downstairs with the kids.

Without any of us feeling the time slip away, it suddenly dawns on us that it's nearly 4 o' clock. We've had sandwiches together, played a game of Simon Says, and spent all afternoon talking about Addie, Madge, and seemingly every detail of our own lives.

"I'm so sorry; I didn't intend to stay all day," Violet profusely apologizes as she begins rounding up her children and getting them into their shoes.

"No, I *wanted* you to stay," I assure her. "I needed this so much."

"You all are so sweet! I *loved* spending the day with you all," I beam as I bend down at eye level to the youngest ones.

Violet smiles before leaning close and whispering, "If I'd brought my two littlest boys, they'd have been swinging from the light fixtures and sliding down the stair railing…they don't do so well indoors..."

Violet and I share a laugh.

"That would have been perfectly fine. You should bring them next time; I don't mind," I promise.

"We'll see…" Violet replies. "Luckily John is chopping lots of firewood today and they're running wild and free within his eyesight."

The thought of Joseph chopping firewood while our children play in the woods and around the farm delights me. I wish he were home to meet Violet and her kids.

Suddenly I go against the best judgment and enter an attitude of boldness.

"Do you have plans for this weekend?" I ask, feeling uncomfortably vulnerable but somehow unbothered by it.

"Actually, no," Violet responds. "John is off this weekend, but we aren't doing anything special. What do you have in mind?"

"Oh, I don't know. Anything," I say with a shrug.

"I have an idea! Have you ever eaten at the Green Canteen?" Violet asks.

"Hmmm. I've passed by it, but I've never been there," I answer.

"Well, I was thinking that if John doesn't mind staying home with all the kids for a bit, you and I could go and have lunch. Just the two of us."

"Yes! I'm off Friday, and Joseph will be working. Will that work?" I ask, hopeful.

"Sure," she replies. "I'll let you know once I ask John, but I don't think he will mind. I never go anywhere alone, and he's so good with the children. They love spending time with him."

"Oh, good. It's a date, then," I reply with a smile.

As the van pulls out of the driveway, I stand on the porch and wave the way Grandmama always did every time someone departed from our old farmhouse. I smile to myself as I turn and head back inside. The warm house and Dill are equally inviting as I step inside.

"Oh, Dilly boy!" I squeal as I rub his ears. "We had company, didn't we? Wasn't that fun?"

The kitchen soon begins to produce savory, spicy aromas that fill the house as I stir the pot of chili beans on the stove top. Joseph will be home shortly, and I can hardly wait to tell him about my day.

I reflect on the past several hours as I prepare supper in the little old kitchen, seasoned by time and the overseeing of countless creations. The best things seem to happen to me when I least expect it, I realize as I set the table.

This house appeared on the market in the midst of a prolonged mental depression, when I was sure my life would never see another moment of happiness. Of course there was Addie, shortly after, who came to my aid and offered solace through the words written on the pages of her diary. Then, Joseph fled in and positively swooped me off my feet, to say the least. And now, I've found myself in disbelief once again at the crossing of my path with Violet's. More and more, I find myself realizing that there's no such thing as happenstance. There can't be.

My moment of deep reflection and gratitude nearly causes me to ignore Joseph's entrance through the front door. At the sound of the door closing shut, I startle and turn to greet him, holding a glass full of ice in each hand.

"Hey! You scared me," I admit with a giggle.

"I'm sorry," he says, wearing a weary smile. He crosses the living room with his large lunch tote hanging from his shoulder. I take the bag and toss it onto the counter before folding inside his arms.

"How was your day?" I ask.

"It was actually pretty good," he replies, brushing my hair out of my face.

"Nobody did anything stupid today," he clarifies with a chuckle.

"And how was yours?" he asks.

"Amazing," I declare. "It went by so quickly, but it really was a great day."

As we sit for supper, I begin to tell him about Violet and the children.

"You won't believe it," I say, between blowing on a spoonful of soup.

"Well, tell me," he says.

"Violet got here and was looking around kind of strangely, right? And then she says she *knew Addie*. Do you *believe* that?"

I continue without waiting for his response. "And it gets better. Not only did she know Addie, but… do you remember me talking about Madge, Addie's best friend?"

Joseph obviously strains his memory as he scoops chili onto a corn chip.

"Uh, maybe?" he finally says.

Ignoring his forgetfulness or prior lack of attentiveness, I continue.

"Well, she wrote a lot about Madge in all of her diaries, pretty much. *Anyway,* guess what. Violet. Is. Madge's. Daughter."

I pause and wait for him to gasp and choke on his food at my shocking revelation, but neither happens. Instead, he raises his eyebrows slightly as he takes another bite.

"Really?" he asks. "That's crazy."

I can't control my urge to laugh at his indifference.

"I can tell you're shaken to the core," I reply.

"Isn't that wild, though? I never would have imagined this happening. It's such a small world, and you *know* how I feel about using that phrase in a small town," I chuckle.

"Yeah, it is really cool," he admits with a smile playing on his lips.

"And what's more? Violet and I spent all day talking, and I can imagine us being the closest of friends. I miss Jill like crazy, but I enjoyed Violet's company so much."

"Well, that's good. I'm happy for you," Joseph replies. And I know that he deeply means it, despite his placidity.

"So, what is she like?" he asks.

"Oh, just wonderful and her kids are just wonderful too. She said that Addie delivered three of them and I just wanted to cry when she told me."

I continue quickly. "She stays home and raises babies and cooks everything from scratch while her husband, John, works at some kind of manufacturing plant – I can't remember exactly – but she homeschools the kids, and she seems to do so well with them. You can just feel the ease, like she was born for it…"

Joseph just smiles across the table as I continue.

"Oh, and guess what…We're going out for lunch on Friday."

Joseph nods. "That'll be fun," he comments.

"Yeah, I'm pretty excited. I should text Jill and tell her about all this, shouldn't I?"

"If you want to," Joseph replies, still grinning.

"I will, maybe tonight. She'll be as stunned as I am," I mumble more to myself than to Joseph.

As soon as supper is finished and the table is cleared away, Joseph walks up to me from behind and wraps his arms around my waist.

"I'm happy you've found Violet," he finally says.

"Don't you go forgetting about me though, you hear?" he whispers into my ear with a soft chuckle.

I spin around to face him. "Forget about you…how could I?"

SIX

Once again, quite some time has passed between my journaling. This time, because I've been so busy that in the evenings, I'm worn out and ready for sleep. I've assisted with the birth of five babies since I've last written. They were all healthy babies, calm births, and happy mamas. I cannot ask for more than that.

Between all of my appointments with my expectant mothers, milking Ginger, tending to the gardens and animals, and attending births, I've found I do not possess an excess of free time. However, there's always time for Madge.

She dropped in this morning, bringing a stack of magazines and a strawberry pie.

"I can assure you, these are my berries I'd frozen from the summer....not those tainted with all sorts of chemical sprays," she clarified as she sat the dessert on the kitchen table. I made her a cup of apple mint tea – her favorite – and we sat on the porch and enjoyed the *bliss of an early autumn morning...my very favorite season of all.*

Springtime offers a sweet awakening of the earth after a season of cold, dark dormancy. The daffodils show up first, as if to introduce the rest of the impending burst of life coming forth. The blossoms and leaves slowly appear, adding a touch of pastel color to our world. The lavender-colored wisteria blossoms hang from trees around the farm, draped like peppery-scented blankets of grape-like clusters. The birds' songs are merry, and the air is a touch warmer, offering the promise of a bountiful summer ahead.

Winter creeps in slowly and seems to last longer than its actual passage of time. The bare, naked trees find rest but once a year and the world seems to hush and hibernate along with them. Cold, seemingly lifeless but merely buried in the task of reposing in preparation for the seasons of bearing fruits. Like an author, who on the surface seems still and vacant, but is only inwardly preparing for the fruits of his labor to bloom in due course.

Summer is vibrant and full of life that bursts forth with vigorous warmth and color. Bold aromas scent the air around me as the gardenias and roses bloom in all their beauty. The foxgloves and peonies decorate the front path with familiar pastel blooms. The tastes are like none other...fresh, ripe, robust. A bountiful harvest erupts as the days get longer and warmer, until finally they seem to melt and run into the next one. Tanned skin tells the story of one who has tasted and seen the magnificence of nature on a long summer's day. The night air is thick, and the frogs' chorus offers songs for the weary as they retire in the nautical-blue evening…a day's work completed to the soul's satisfaction.

And then, there's autumn…the best one. A time that is simultaneously exhilarating and relaxing. The satisfying, yet tiresome season of summer comes to a close, early autumn offering little bits of rewards for the work put in. A few late harvests continue to stray in – enough to enjoy and sustain but not to overwhelm with the task of preserving and preparing in haste. The slightest nip in the air comes as a sweet respite as beautiful goldenrod erupts in the fields and dances in the first chilly gust. The trees' leaves display stunning shades of copper and then bronze before they let them go, where they'll heap into crisp hills around the dark, bare trunks. The mountains glow as if they're ablaze for only a short while, their beauty a breathtaking reminder of the miracle of Creation.

The smells of cinnamon and nutmeg fill my home as I enjoy hot teas, spicy, comforting desserts, and hearty soups. During this time, when the pantry is filled with the summer's plentiful harvests and the firewood is stacked neatly in abundance by the front door, I begin to put my mind and body to rest a bit.

I especially love autumn births. I find myself spending the "golden hour" in the crisp outdoors while the new mother basks in the intoxicating relief with her new baby folded snugly against her chest. Once they are settled and safe, I will make the mother a nourishing soup, a hot cup of tea or broth, and offer her a pair of warm knit socks.

I have two mothers nearing the end of their pregnancies, but neither are likely to deliver for the next few weeks. Today, after Madge brought the scrumptious (pesticide free) offering, she and I had a wonderful day together. As we sat on the porch in the still of the late morning, we had wonderful, unhurried conversations. Her daughter, sweet Violet, is growing so fast; when she gets home from school, Madge spends the rest of the afternoon and evening nurturing and attending Violet's every need, as a doting and loving mother.

Madge welcomed Violet later in life. I remember vividly, the night she gave birth to her. She was so afraid something would go wrong because she was well into her forties. Of course, I reassured her every day for eight months that there was absolutely no reason to fear such. Though I don't think she fully believed me until after the birth, Madge was still very adamant that I be the one to deliver her baby. To which I gladly obliged, of course.

Madge did have a long, tough labor, but she did wonderfully and received the reward of a beautiful, healthy, red-headed baby girl. Violet is still such a pretty young girl, and so smart. I enjoy it very much when she comes with Madge for a visit.

After talking for a while, Madge and I decided to dine out together for lunch. We hadn't done so in quite some time, so we decided to drive up the mountain a piece, to our favorite restaurant, The Green Canteen. It's the only restaurant for miles around that doesn't serve mystery meat on an herbicide-laced, preservative-filled bun with a side of almost-potatoes fried in who-knows-what overprocessed inflammatory cooking oil.

The curvy drive up the mountain to the restaurant in the small village was peaceful and beautiful. The trees' yellow and orange leaves illuminated the forests and offered a comforting glow while the bluegrass music played softly on Madge's car radio.

The restaurant was lively, as always. The softly lit dining room was full of laughter, conversations, and the clinking of silverware. I enjoyed every bite of my "usual"... I always have the rosemary-garlic elk steak & Madge, her mustard-cream rabbit with wild rice.

Afterwards, we shared a piece of double dark chocolate cake, per tradition. And as we paid the bill at the large, outdated cash register up front, Madge bought two peppermint patties as a treat for Violet...per tradition.

She couldn't wait to pick her up from school...she said she might even check her out a little early, "since it's Friday", and take her to pick out a small gift at our local Wal-Mart. I hope she will bring her by to visit soon.

In the meantime, I plan to turn inward in synchrony with nature. To store up my energy for the spring. In addition to attending a few wonderful, miraculous births spaced out over the fall and winter, I'll read, journal, pore over frame-worthy puzzles, sip clove tea with the cat purring softly on my lap by the fire. Just a bit of dilly-dally. And I look forward to it with earnestness.

SEVEN

The deafening sound of my phone ringing from the nightstand startles me awake. I open one eyelid enough to see that it's still dark. Who would be calling this time of morning?

The words "The Home" dance across the bright screen beneath **5:51 AM**, as the ringing continues. Joseph doesn't stir.

Work calling me at this time of morning can only mean one thing…someone has called in and they want to beg me to come in on my day off.

"Ugh," I moan as I silence the call.

Rubbing my tender eyes, I sit up and look over at Joseph in the light of the glowing lamp in the corner. He's still sound asleep.

I swing my feet to the floor and quietly tiptoe out of the room and to the bathroom, taking my phone with me. Once the door is shut, I stare at the phone for several seconds before scrolling to the last call.

As it rings, I ponder hanging up. It's not too late.

"*Sunny Meadows?*" says Sharon after just two rings. I could still just hang up.

"Hey, it's Blaire," I groggily answer instead.

"Oh, *hey,*" Sharon says, seemingly relieved.

"Anne just called in sick, and I was wondering if you'd be willing to cover the shift today. She was scheduled for 100-wing."

Ordinarily, I wouldn't even answer the phone, let alone consider this nonsense.

"Um…Yeah, I guess I can," I blurt before I have the chance to change my mind.

I don't know what's come over me. It's almost as if I actually care about the inconveniences of my co-workers. Surely Violet's kindness toward others isn't rubbing off on me *this* soon.

After pulling my hair back and throwing on a solid black pair of scrubs, I brush my teeth and splash my face with water.

I hate to wake Joseph on his day off; he seems to be sleeping so well. Tiptoeing back down the short hallway and into the bedroom, I quietly fumble around in the dimly lit bedroom for a pen and piece of paper from the large desk in the corner.

I quickly scribble a note to him as best I can by the lamp light and attach it onto the ceiling fan pull above the bed. I keep a clothespin in the nightstand drawer especially for this purpose.

"Got called in to work. I should be home around 4. Love you. -B," it reads.

Joseph and Dill are both knocked out and snoring like a couple of hibernating bears underneath the covers. I should still be in bed with them, I think to myself as I leave the room and softly pad down the stairs to the kitchen.

I'm doing a favor today, so I really don't need to be in too much of a rush; however, I also don't want to be behind with all the morning medications, so I take a homemade English muffin from the bread box and fill it with a piece of leftover bacon to eat in the car. Quickly, I brew a single serving of coffee into my stainless-steel coffee thermos and give it a good glug of half and half before pulling on my sweater and quietly opening the front door.

The air outside is frigid, but the sun is beginning to peek over the horizon. The rooster crows as I walk across the frosty grass toward the car. I can see my breath in the cool morning air, and I think of Addie's description of each season. The purpose and beauty in each one, the perspective which she described them from. It almost makes me ashamed of myself for loathing winter so much.

The long stretch of highway leading to the crooked driveway of *Sunny Meadows* seems shorter today, for some reason. I realize, as I pull up the hill toward the large brick home with windows aglow, that I've spent the entire drive thinking of Addie and Violet. The threads that hold the story together are the unlikeliest, yet wonderfully true. I can't wait to talk to Violet and tell her about her mom and Addie going to the Green Canteen.

I climb the splintery wooden stairs and enter the heavy door right into the nurses' station, where I find Sharon making notes in a patient's chart, as fast as her fingers will write. She looks up as I enter through the door and place my bag on the wooden desk just inside it.

"Hey," she says, smiling. The sight of me entering the room means that Sharon is nearly relieved of her nursing duties for this shift. She probably also feared that she'd have to stay over if she couldn't find anyone to agree to come in.

"Hey," I mumble before taking a sip of coffee and pulling up a chair across from her at the large oak table that looks as if it once belonged in someone's dining room.

"How was the night?" I ask.

"Oh, it was fine," Sharon answers, tucking her pen into her pocket.

"You'll never guess who came back while you were gone," she says with wide eyes.

"Who?" I ask.

"Mrs. White," Sharon answers as she awaits my shocked reaction.

"The Mrs. White that I performed CPR on last week?" I ask, puzzled.

"Yep," Sharon confirms with a look of satisfaction.

"Feeding tube and all," she adds in a sing-song voice.

"No, way," I reply. "Are you serious?"

"See for yourself. It's pitiful if you ask me," she says, nodding down the long corridor toward room 109.

"Well, that's wild," I utter as I sit in disbelief.

"Does Cindy know? She was with me during the code blue."

"Yeah. She's proud, though. She's going around telling people that she revived Mrs. White and yada yada…" Sharon rolls her eyes as she mimics Cindy.

"Wow. That kind of surprises me from Cindy. I wouldn't have thought she'd have that kind of attitude about something like that," I say, my mind flashing back to Cindy and I attempting to restart Mrs. White's tired, old heart.

"Me, neither! It shocked me, but I'm getting sick of hearing about it. Everyone is. Just wait until she gets here. You'll get to hear it all day long," Sharon says with a snicker.

I shake my head in disbelief, at both the fact that Mrs. White has returned to the facility and that Cindy is bragging about it.

"Oh, well," I finally say with a sigh. I look around for a scrap of paper to write down the report on just as the heavy door opens and a gust of cold air blows in.

"Well, *good morning,* Blaire!" Cindy exclaims as she enters the room.

"I didn't know *you* were working with us today! This is my right-hand woman, Sharon," Cindy says as she gives my shoulder a squeeze.

"Blaire, did she tell you about Mrs. White?"

Here we go. I steal a glance at Sharon as I scribble the date on my paper. She gives me a knowing look with the faintest trickle of a smile.

"Yes, I did," Sharon answers.

"Isn't that awesome news, Blaire?" Cindy asks. "She made it!"

I force a smile. "Yeah, that's wild isn't it?"

Cindy is oblivious in regard to my sarcasm as she hops out of the room and around the corner to the time clock, her large cup of tea in hand.

"She must start drinking that sweet tea as soon as her feet hit the floor," I whisper to Sharon, who covers her mouth to stifle a laugh.

I shiver as I watch Cindy place a plastic-wrapped breakfast bagel in the microwave and press the start button. After nuking the bioengineered food-like ingredients with plastic particles and high-frequency radiation, the bagel will have the nutritional value of a piece of cardboard. And she'd probably be better off eating cardboard, for that matter.

Once Sharon has reported the events of the night to me, and I've filled my medicine cart with the juices and puddings I'll use to administer medications with, I head down the dim 100-wing to peek at each patient, or at least listen for them to snore, the wall sconce lamps and residents' televisions lighting the way for me.

In and out of the rooms I dart, back and forth across the hallway. Meg has begun getting some of the patients up and ready for the day. Mrs. Crawford and Mrs. Henson are both sitting in their wheelchairs, wearing their cardigans and watching the morning news with the television volume on ninety-thousand decibels.

"Good morning!" I shout. I add a wave, because they still likely didn't hear me.

"Beulah, turn it *down!*" yells Mrs. Henson with a frown.

"*What!?*" Mrs. Crawford shouts back.

"*Turn. It. Dow*—- Nurse, honey, would you turn that down?" Mrs. Henson asks, pointing to the television.

I pick the remote control up from Mrs. Crawford's bed and hold the volume button down for several seconds. It's still loud enough to be heard in the next room.

"Is that better?" I ask.

"What were you saying? I couldn't hear nothing but that blame television. Beulah wants to keep it turned all the way up!" Mrs. Henson sputters, shaking her head.

I giggle and mimic Mrs. Henson's headshaking. "I was just saying good morning!"

"Oh, well good morning to you." Mrs. Henson nods and looks a bit annoyed that that's all I wanted.

She's forgotten that I do the same thing nearly every morning.

"And I wanted to see if you had a copy of yesterday's newspaper I could borrow?" I lie.

At this, Mrs. Henson scurries in her wheelchair to the basket next to her quilted bed.

"Uh-huh, it's around here somewhere, honey," she says cheerfully.

She clumsily sifts through her books and magazines before discovering a wrinkled newspaper, which she opens and starts flipping through.

"I just want the puzzles and the obituary page. You can have the rest," she says as she hands me the folded paper.

"Thank you!" I exclaim. "I'll bring it back if you want."

"No, no. You keep it. I've already read it. This is all I want." She holds up the two sheets of newspaper.

"I've got to see who's died in Weatherford," she says, tucking the folded papers onto her lamp-lit bedside table until downtime after Bingo this afternoon.

I stifle a laugh. "Okay, well thank you, Mrs. Henson! I'll be in with your medicine shortly."

I turn to walk out of the room when Mrs. Crawford stops me.

"Wait! nurse?" she calls.

"Yes?" I turn to face her as she tries to quickly maneuver her wheelchair around the bed and over to her bedside table. There, she turns on her lamp and begins raking through a tin box before producing a butterscotch candy in a yellow wrapper and holding it out toward me.

"Here, honey," she says. "Have a little piece of candy."

"I'm sweet enough, aren't I?" I tease before taking the candy from her soft, arthritic hand.

She chuckles with a wink, apparently satisfied for the moment.

"Thank you," I say as I leave the room, tucking the candy into my scrub pocket. I might have to use it later to bribe Mr. Sanders into wearing his compression stockings.

Back and forth across the darkened corridor I continue until I reach the one I've been dreading. Lamp light floods into the hallway from the opened door at the end of it. I approach it slowly, a mechanical whirring sound growing louder with each step.

In the window bed, lies a frail, 80-pound woman who tried to die with dignity in this very bed, but instead is being assaulted with violent interventions that keep her "alive". I feel partly responsible. First, I found she wasn't breathing, and, per doctor's orders and family's wishes, I initiated CPR. Needles and tubes were jammed into her body, more compressions, more broken ribs. I never thought she'd make it to the ambulance.

Powerful medications were administered for days via more needles, more tubes. Somehow, she was deemed stable enough by some dimwit, to have a major operation in order to place a feeding tube into her stomach because she wasn't eating. By a "miracle", she came through the surgery and received more strong medications while she laid in the hospital bed, lethargic and unable to communicate her wants or needs.

After five more days in the hospital, she was released back to her room at *Sunny Meadows,* her daughter, Donna, close behind - no doubt. I'm surprised she isn't here now, as a matter of fact. If she were, I'd be forced to resist the urge to take her by the shoulders and shake her, shouting, "Let her go, you selfish woman!"

The shell of a body lies still, other than the shallow rise and fall of her chest. Her gray hair hasn't been washed in weeks, but at least it has been combed. Her mouth and eyes are open, but she doesn't see me. Hanging from the metal pole above her, is the jug of formula that's intermittently being pumped directly into Mrs. White's stomach via an open wound. The sound the pump makes as it feeds the thick, brown liquid through the plastic tubing makes my skin crawl.

I lean closer to the feeding pump and glance at the ingredient list on the jug of formula. I shiver as I scan the list of toxic, inflammatory ingredients in a product that's designed to sustain a minimally functioning body. On the headboard of her bed, there is a square, purple sticker that reads "Full Scope of Treatment." When her body eventually gives out for good, we are supposed to attempt the whole thing over again.

In the meantime, nursing staff will administer her many medications via her stomach tube, hang a new jug of the formula each time it empties, change her adult diaper every couple of hours, and manually reposition her body routinely to prevent bed sores. And when she does inevitably develop bed sores, we will begin a treatment plan for her painful wounds, add the high protein option to her corn syrup/seed oil slurry, and increase her pain medication.

I look down at the worn-out body with pale, almost transparent skin stretched across visible bones, and Addie's voice comes to my mind. I can almost hear her audibly, say…

"Just because we *can* doesn't mean we *should*."

I place my hand on Mrs. White's head and softly stroke her silver hair. She continues to stare into space, but I think I can see the faintest trickle of a smile at the corner of her mouth. A tear slips down my cheek and drops onto the floor, as I wonder who she was when she was healthy, full of life, able to make decisions for herself. I'm certain she wouldn't choose to spend the last months of her life enduring all of this nonsensical brutality.

After staying with Mrs. White for longer than I'd planned to, combing her hair and ensuring that she looked as comfortable as possible, I finally managed to begin my morning round. From my place in front of the giant medicine cart, the smell of bacon beginning to swirl around as breakfast is prepared, I can hear Mrs. Crawford and Mrs. Henson arguing again. I think all is right on this end of the hall.

EIGHT

"It's ludicrous, Joseph. To be honest, I dread even going back to work this weekend."

I stir my tea, the spoon clinking against the inside of my mug.

"Don't go," Joseph answers with a shrug.

"Be serious," I retort, rolling my eyes.

"I *am* serious. Don't go. You don't *have* to, you know. We can afford for you to stay at home, if you want."

"You make everything seem so simple," I say as I take a seat on the couch next to Dill.

"Well, it *is* pretty simple, if you ask me," he says, joining us. "Do you love it? Do you see yourself nursing for the rest of your life?"

I ponder his question seriously before answering.

"I used to love it. But, no…I can't see myself doing it forever," I finally answer, picking at the afghan on my lap.

"What *can* you see yourself doing, then?"

"Oh, I don't know," I answer, looking up at him. "It's just what I'm *good* at. The only skills I have are put to use in that building. I know just what to do and I do it well…But seeing my patient like that infuriates me. It makes me want no part of any of it. And also, it makes me want to have a will drawn up, like *today*."

"We'll write a will, then," he replies with a smile. "By the way, those aren't the only skills you have. But if you wanted to, you could always learn a new skill. And as for the rest of it, try not to worry. You're off tomorrow…and you get to go out with Violet, right? Isn't that tomorrow?"

"You're right, I know. I'm really excited about seeing Violet, too. We texted a little bit today when I wasn't too busy at work."

"Good," he says. "The ball is in your court. Remember that."

I watch him as he pushes off the back of the couch and heads into the kitchen for his coffee.

"What did I ever do to deserve you?"

"What are you talking about?" he asks. "I think it should be the other way around."

"You're always adding an 'if you want to' and I know you just want me to be happy. Which I absolutely am," I add.

"I hope so," he replies as he stirs his coffee.

Suddenly, there is a knock at the door. Both of us jump and look toward the front door.

I gasp at the sight of our unexpected guest through the window at the door.

"It's Violet!" I exclaim, rising from the couch. Dill lifts his head and perks his ears.

I swiftly cross the small living room and open the door, with Joseph trailing behind me.

"Hey!" I greet her. "Come in!"

"I'm so sorry to drop by unannounced. I'm heading out to the dairy to pick up our herd share milk, and I had something I wanted to give you."

"Don't apologize, I'm glad you're here!" I say, beaming.

"Joseph, this is my friend, Violet," I happily introduce them.

"And this is the one I can't do without," I say, nodding toward Joseph.

I smile as I stand between them, waiting for them to speak to each other.

"So nice to meet you!" Violet chirps with an outstretched hand.

Joseph shakes her hand a bit awkwardly and replies, "Nice to meet you, too. I've heard a lot about you." He snickers nervously as he looks back and forth between Violet and I. Then, he takes a seat on the nearby couch.

"Well!" Violet snaps, turning to me. "I won't stay. I just brought you something, like I said! Some things I wanted you to have."

She pulls a glass jelly jar from her coat pocket and offers it to me, the sound of something rattling inside. As I hold it up, I see that it's nearly full of seashells. Different shapes and colors but all small in size with bits of blue and green sea glass mixed in with them.

I smile at the beauty of the shells before Violet speaks up. "Mom and Addie found those along the coast at Lovespring Island. Their favorite thing to do together at the beach was to go shelling."

I glance at Violet, in awe of the special gift in my hands. "Oh, Violet…Thank you. These will be treasured forever," I utter, turning the jar and watching the shells and glass tumble inside.

"My goodness, this is special. I *love* shells, but *these*…Just, wow."

"You're most welcome! But I do have one more thing for you," Violet says as she reaches back inside her coat pocket.

"Hold out your hand," she says, holding something small between her thumb and index finger.

As I do so, she places a small, golden ring in my palm. I hold it up and examine it closely, immediately recognizing it. Two small golden hands cradling a heart-shaped emerald.

I look up at Violet. "Addie's claddagh ring?" I ask, my voice cracking a bit.

Violet slowly nods and offers a knowing smile. "She wore that ring for as long as I can remember. It looked so pretty and dainty on her finger…a daily reminder of her heritage."

"Are you sure you want to give this away?"

"For you, I'm sure," Violet answers. "To be honest, I never thought I'd get rid of either of these things, but then I never thought any of this would happen." Violet motions between herself and I, laughing softly.

Then she continues, "Mom left everything to me when she passed, and they were among the things I couldn't bear to part with. But don't worry…there are many more things I couldn't part with!"

"Well, I don't know how I could thank you for this."

"You already have, with that diary you gave me. I started reading it right away, and you were right! Addie wrote about Mom in the very first entry…the very first page, even. Oh, it's been so heartwarming and heartbreaking to read, both at the same time."

"I'll bet so," I reply. I know how much *I* love reading Addie's diaries. I can't imagine how special it must be for you."

"It's really amazing. Thank you again," Violet says, backing toward the door.

"I'd better get going, though. I have my oldest two in the car waiting."

She turns toward Joseph in his spot on the couch and throws her hand up. "Joseph, it was nice meeting you. Sorry again, to barge in like this."

"You're welcome to come by anytime you like," Joseph answers with a bashful grin.

"Oh, we're still on for lunch tomorrow, right?" Violet blurts as she suddenly turns back to me.

"I can't wait," I answer, beaming.

"I'm even more excited since reading Addie's last journal entry. I'll tell you about it tomorrow!"

"Now, I'm *curious*," Violet says, eyes wide. But she reaches for the door latch.

I follow Violet out the door and turn the porch light on.

"I can't wait to tell you all about it," I say, hugging myself in the chilly night air.

"Me either!" Violet says, walking briskly down the porch steps.

"I'll be here to pick you up at eleven!" she calls from the darkened front yard.

"See you then!" I yell with a wave.

Back inside, I close the door behind me and look down at my pinky finger, adorned with the most beautiful treasure. I run my finger over the emerald, tracing the tiny facets and the grooves of the simple gold embellishments. Emotions try to peak as I comprehend where the ring has been and where it is now. It feels like such a full-circle moment as I proudly wear Addie's special ring, right here in Addie's home.

The day's frustrations melt away as I look up to see Joseph watching me silently from the couch, his coffee cup in hand. He smiles a knowing smile, locking my glassy eyes.

"It looks good on you, honey."

NINE

"It's a little embarrassing to admit how excited I've been for you to pick me up."

Violet laughs as she adjusts the heat in her van. "Don't worry. I've been looking forward to today, too!"

I hold my hand out in front of us, revealing Addie's ring.

"It fits my pinky finger perfectly. And I'll probably never take it off," I say, smiling.

"I'm so glad you love it. I was hoping you would, although it surprised me how quickly you recognized that it belonged to Addie," Violet says.

"It's ironic – which, what isn't anymore? – but one of the last things I've read from Addie's diary was about this very ring. She was talking about how much it meant to her because her mother had given it to her when she was just a little girl." My eyes feel the stinging threat of tears before I force them away.

"That is really something else, isn't it?" Violet smiles as she drives up the curvy mountain road.

"Where exactly was Addie from originally?" I ask.

"Well, I'm not sure of the precise location, but she and her family were from a little village in Ireland. Even from a young age, Addie used to help her mother with births in their Irish village, as well as treating the sick with herbal remedies. From what I've been told, Addie's mother was very bright and was loved by all the members of their community," Violet says.

"Do you know what caused them to come here?" I ask, hungry for knowledge about Addie.

"All I really know is that they came here when Addie was still pretty young…about ten or so, I think? The house you live in was their family's house. Addie grew up there."

The story of Addie continues to get sweeter, penetrating my soul and offering bits of comfort that I can tuck away for a rainy day.

"*Really?*" I ask, pleasantly surprised. "Addie hasn't really journaled much about her parents or her childhood."

"Yep…Addie never moved out. She grew up, became a midwife, married Isaiah, and had a son, all while staying in the home and taking care of her parents until they died. I know it seems kind of strange, her not wanting to have her own home with her own family. But, as you may have gathered, Addie was a bit of the eccentric type, anyway. She did things her own way. Don't get me wrong– she was *amazing*. She was kind of the 'black sheep' everywhere she went, ya know? It didn't bother her, though…"

Violet pauses for a moment as I cling to every word.

"Mr. Isaiah was so head over heels for Addie, he didn't care where they lived. He learned a lot from Addie's parents and eventually came to love them like they were his own…they both passed away the same year, which was right around Addie and Isaiah's fifteenth wedding anniversary – I know all of this only from years' worth of being in the center of Mom and Addie's conversations," Violet adds with a snicker.

"I sure am glad you were!" I'm soaking up every bit of it.

"Did you know Addie's son?" I ask, remembering the painfully grievous pages I have read about Michael's death and Addie's mourning.

"Actually, no," Violet says. "See, Addie was about ten years older than Mom. And she had Michael at a fairly young age, while Mom had *me* later in life…so by the time I was born, Michael was grown. He passed away while I was still too young to remember him."

"Oh, *wait!* You had something to tell me, didn't you? I'm so sorry," Violet says.

"No, it's okay. I do want to tell you before we get to the restaurant though, because it's very relevant." I chuckle.

Violet grins in excitement as we wind closer to the town of Bascomb.

"Okay, so…did you know Addie and Madge used to go to the Green Canteen together?" I ask.

"Yeah," Violet answers. "It was their favorite spot." She says it calmly, as if she's reflecting fondly on days past.

"I thought it was so ironic to read about the two of them going out to eat there right after you mentioned the place to me. In the diary, Addie had written that they'd gone out for lunch…you were at school…and she said she had her usual – elk steak, and your Mom always had some kind of rabbit dish with wild rice."

Violet chuckles. "That's right," she says. "The mustard cream rabbit."

"Oh yeah, that's it," I agree.

As we get closer to the restaurant, I begin to feel a little nervous for reasons I'm unsure of. Will being there cause me to be emotional? And what about Violet? Surely old memories will flood in. It *was* her idea to come here, though. Maybe she frequents the Green Canteen.

"Do you go to this restaurant a lot?" I ask.

"Oh, no. I cook all of our meals at home. We like it better that way; besides, can you see me bringing six children to a restaurant very often?" Violet laughs at the thought.

"I guess not," I agree with a chuckle. "I was just wondering. I hope it doesn't make you sad or anything…you know, remembering your Mom and Addie being there so many times."

"Well, I don't have to go to the Green Canteen to remember Mom. I think of her every single day, for one reason or the other. This might as well be today's reminder," Violet says with an air of certainty.

"I honestly can't believe you grew up here and have never eaten there before, though." Violet chuckles.

"Any time Daddy decided to treat Grandmama and I with a supper out, we'd always go to the fish camp." I laugh as I remember riding in the old pickup truck between the two of them, the smoke from Daddy's cigarette swirling around us, mingling with the scent of greasy seafood on our clothes.

"The fish camp out on Loudy Road?" Violet asks.

"Yeah, that's the one!" I answer. "Are they even still in business? I haven't been out that way in *years*."

"I'm not sure, but I think so. Maybe we should take the long way home and ride by it, if you want."

"That'd be fun," I reply. "It'll be a trip down memory lane, either way."

Slowly, we approach the town, with both sides of the street lined with familiar stores, an ice cream shoppe, and the entry gate to tour the widely known *Bascomb Cavern*. Finally, we arrive in front of the two-story stucco destination. It looks just as I remember it, in my years' worth of passing through town. A green-painted wrought iron banister curves around the corner of the building, draped with English Ivy and leading to the upstairs portion of the restaurant. In the upstairs windows, electric candlesticks flicker and glow a false orange fire, visible in the overcast day.

"They look crowded, as usual," says Violet as we circle the building in search of a parking spot.

"Must be a popular place," I comment, scanning the lot.

"This'll do," she says, pulling into a space beneath a naked-branched tree.

Inside, the place is humming, just as Addie described it so many years ago.

Everywhere I look, glass eyes from various stuffed animals look back at me; the taxidermists' dream. The atmosphere is one that's comforting and friendly, though. The smell of peppers and onions fill the carpeted dining room. Chatter and laughter seem to bounce off the walls and friendly smiles pass by, one right after the other. The warm-natured hostess greets us with hospitality, asking our preferences and party number.

"The smell is mouthwatering," I comment as we take our seats. "The scent of peppers and onions cooking always reminds me of the indoor flea market Daddy and I used to go to," I say with a chuckle. The mental picture of a red and white *Boiled Peanuts* sign flashes before my eyes.

"Isn't it funny how a certain smell takes you right back to an exact time or place, no matter how long it's been?" Violet asks.

"Yeah…but I love that. I wouldn't trade my special memories for anything in the world."

I slowly glance around, imagining Addie and Madge in this very dining room, perhaps at this very table by the window with the view of the Bascomb River gorge below.

"I don't know about you," Violet says, looking over the thick paper menu. "But, I don't think I need this menu…I'll have to have the mustard cream rabbit with wild rice. For Mom." She smiles as she pushes the menu away.

"Well, in that case I'll just have to have the elk steak," I declare.

"We've gotta, don't we?" Violet asks.

"We've gotta," I agree.

During the wait for our honorary meals, the conversation flows fluidly. I could easily sit and talk to Violet all day long. About Addie, or about anything at all.

"Well…tell me more about you, about your background," Violet says, pulling her knit cardigan tightly around her.

"Me?" I ask, startled. "There's not much to tell about *me*."

"Sure, there is. What was your childhood like? Tell me about your parents."

Now, there's something I could talk about for days on end. My childhood. The days I reflect on so much that they seem like my identity, and I know I'll carry them for eternity.

I giggle as I ponder on where to begin.

"Well…I lived on a farm where my Daddy and Grandmama raised me. See, my mother died when I was a baby, and I have no memory of her whatsoever."

Violet listens intently as I pour out the deepest, most sacred parts of myself. Like breaking off a piece of my innermost being and laying it on the table between us, to share for a bit, before tucking it back inside for safe keeping.

"I had the most wonderful childhood, Violet. Although I was an only child, there was no shortage of love, or excitement, or joy…every day. Grandmama– that was Daddy's Mama – she looked after the house…and me… and Daddy too, I guess. She was almost *always* in the kitchen preparing food in abundance, with the radio playing from its place on the counter. She was a merry flame burning at the center of our household."

"And Daddy…well there isn't adequate time or words to describe him," I say, beaming at the memory of his face. "Charlie Whitfield was one of a kind."

"Well, try," Violet says. "If he was that extraordinary, I'd like to hear about him."

"He was. Oh, he was," I reply as I stare across the dim, crowded dining room.

"Daddy was a cattle farmer…" I begin. "But we also had lots of customers who would come to the farm and buy eggs and pork from us….as well as some produce. Grandmama would make all the sausage herself, as well as curing the bacon and the hams. In the summer, they'd let me pick the tomatoes and cucumbers and sell them for myself."

"That does sound like a wonderful childhood," Violet comments with a smile.

"I really believe they tried extra hard to make up for the things I *didn't* have, like siblings or a mother. So, they poured into me all the love they could muster, and I felt it to my core. I feel it still."

"That's what I want for my kids…for them to feel my love so strongly that it carries them through life and bubbles over onto their own children. I'd like to have known your Daddy and Grandmama." Violet offers a sympathetic sort of smile.

"They gave me the best life I could've ever asked for. And we didn't have extra money, you know? We always had enough to get by…we had good food on the table, decent clothes to wear, and we always had the best Christmases…but we were never what you'd call 'well-to-do', by any means."

"Did you ever feel lonely?" Violet asks. "You know, being the only child?"

"I actually didn't. But I also didn't know anything different, so I guess I just thought that was a common, normal life. I did have an aunt and uncle on my mother's side of the family. They had one son, my cousin James, who I loved getting to spend time with on occasion. I had two close girlfriends from school who got to come over a lot, too. And then, there were the adults who were always stopping by. A relative, a friend, a customer…there always seemed to be someone hanging around the kitchen table. Grandmama would never let any visitor leave hungry." I smile at the thought, and long for my home to be a place where people flock to and don't ever want to leave.

"How about you?" I want to ask about her father, but I'm afraid to pry.

"I wasn't necessarily *lonely*. Like you said, I didn't really have anything to compare my life to, and I had friends from school, too. Mom and I were so very close, though. I was just always very thankful for her. Plus, we had Addie, and we spent time with her on a weekly basis. That was always such a joy. She was such a sweet and familiar part of my life."

"Oh, this is us," I say, nodding to the waiter approaching our table. He places the steamy, fragrant plates before each of us before checking to see if we have any additional needs.

"This looks so good," I comment, admiring the perfectly seared elk steak and sauteed asparagus on my plate.

"Yours, too. Have you had the rabbit dish before?" I ask.

"I think I had a bite from Mom's plate once. Do you want to try it?"

Violet and I share our meals with each other, both of them being equally delicious.

"It feels so funny, doesn't it? Sitting here, it's almost like we're 'playing' Addie and Madge..." I stifle a laugh.

"It's wild, isn't it? I wonder what they'd say if they could see us right now, having their favorite dishes at their favorite restaurant, talking about them."

"Well, Addie would be like, 'who is that woman with Violet?'"

We both laugh aloud.

"No, something tells me she would know."

Violet pauses and gives a knowing smile.

I grow quiet as I ponder telling Violet what happened on Moving Day last year. Chills cover the back of my neck as I think about it.

Placing my used cloth napkin on the table, I lean forward on my elbows.

"I want to tell you something, but there's a chance you won't believe me," I say.

"Oh, yeah? Violet asks. "Try me."

"Well, on the day that I moved into the farmhouse – *Addie's* farmhouse, though I didn't know that at the time – Joseph was helping me move in, and I was so excited. Like, walking around on cloud nine all morning."

"And then Joseph and I were out in the yard, and we saw a shadow through the window. So, Joseph went inside the house to check, and when he finally resurfaced, he looked like he'd seen a ghost…and apparently he *did*."

I pause as Violet stares at me, intently.

"*What?*" she asks, putting her fork down.

"Yes," I answer. "It really shook both of us up. He came out, pale as a sheet, and said he'd seen a woman with me…that she'd embraced me. But he could tell that I was oblivious."

Violet leans forward with wide eyes as I continue the story.

"It was so scary. It totally ruined my excitement about moving in, and to make it worse, I was afraid Joseph was about to jump ship–we'd *just* started dating when it happened."

"Anyway, I wound up finding a picture of Addie in her old chart from work, where she'd rehabbed after her knee surgery. I took it to him, and he immediately recognized her."

Violet stares, wide-eyed. "I don't even have any words."

"I know," I agree.

"It shook us up pretty hard. So much happened to me during that short period of time, but once I figured out that what Joseph had seen was actually the memory of Addie, I wasn't afraid anymore. Instead, I felt a strong sense of comfort. It truly was such a whirlwind, but I think I've done pretty well with gaining my footing as a wife and sort-of-homemaker."

"Have you seen anything supernatural since then?" Violet asks.

"Nothing," I answer. "Like I said, I just feel comforted in my house. But I do like to imagine that Addie is there with me, ushering me along in my journey of keeping the home beautiful."

Violet smiles but says nothing for a moment.

Then, she leans forward. "You're not a sort-of-homemaker, by the way. I was amazed at how lovely your home looks and feels. It took me at least two years after marrying John to get the hang of things. Plus, you work outside the home!" she seems to suddenly remember.

"Yeah, for now," I trail off.

"What's the matter?" Violet asks. "You're not thinking of quitting, are you?"

I ponder her question before answering.

"Well, lately I've been distraught about things at work, and I'm not so sure about anything anymore."

"Oh, I didn't realize. I think you do a wonderful job as a nurse."

"Well, not to brag, but I think I do a good job, too," I admit with a giggle. "It's not that I don't enjoy the work. I mean, it's really the only thing I can honestly say I'm *skilled* at. I've always been confident in my abilities as a nurse. But I can't shake the fact that something just doesn't feel right anymore."

"Sometimes, things just don't make sense," Violet replies. "I believe whole-heartedly that intuition is a gift, and that we're foolish not to use it."

"I can believe that, too. Sure, I've had my really hard days at work. I've mocked administration and barked insults under my breath regarding ridiculous protocols and policies. But then yesterday, something happened that knocked the wind out of me."

"What is it?" Violet asks with a furrowed brow.

"I guess I should start at the beginning…Just over a week ago, I found my elderly patient without a pulse, not breathing – essentially dead, right? Well, per protocol, because she did not have a Do Not Resuscitate order, I was required to begin the full scope of treatment. In other words, I needed to do 'everything I could to save her'. So, I called in a hand, started CPR, called an ambulance, the whole nine yards. And it was quite ridiculous; I mean, I still have the image of her lifeless body beneath my hands."

"Goodness, that *is* awful," Violet says. "I don't think I could do that kind of work."

"Yeah," I agree. "I felt so dirty about it at the time, because it's my personal belief that the patients should be able to die with a little more dignity than to have someone pounding on their lifeless body, cramming tubes here and there, it's just…ugh." I shiver at the thought.

"And I thought, as the paramedics were wheeling her out the door toward the ambulance, that their further attempts would be futile. Her body would go to the morgue once they arrived at the hospital, her daughter would come in, heartbroken, and gather all of her belongings and thank us all for taking care of her Mama….but that's not how it happened."

Violet continues to look intently at me, hanging onto every word as the waiter takes our empty plates. She wraps her sweater around her shoulders, her fiery red hair glowing against the green fabric.

"Fast-forward to yesterday. The day started off weird from the get-go. And what I mean by that, is that I was called in on my day off, and I actually went in…which never, ever happens. I have never answered or returned calls from work on my day off, except for when my friend Jill worked nights and was on duty."

"So, anyway, I went in yesterday to find that not only did my patient survive, but she then survived a major surgery to place a permanent feeding tube. She's now lying in bed with broken ribs, a serious abdominal wound, and is being kept alive with some sort of vile swill they call nutrition. I'm not sure if her inability to take it by mouth is considered a blessing or a curse."

"That is just terrible, Blaire. I understand why you'd be shaken up about that. I would be too."

"I can't get her off my mind. And, I feel partially responsible. Maybe if I hadn't really tried…"

"No, Blaire. You did what you should have done, what her family's wishes were. You did what any good nurse would've done," Violet says softly.

"Thank you," I reply. "I keep trying to think of it that way. But it's still hard to picture myself doing that line of work for the rest of my life. It can be so emotionally draining."

"What does Joseph say about it?" Violet asks.

"He told me I should quit," I state matter-of-factly.

Violet snickers. "Well…that's an option. How do *you* feel about that?"

"It's been lingering in the back of my mind, I'll admit. And it sounds better and better all the while."

"I'm sure you'll make the right decision," Violet replies.

"Yeah…I guess," I reply.

"So, are you ready, or do you want to have dessert?" she asks.

"As much as I'd love to share a piece of the chocolate cake Addie mentioned, I don't think I can hold it. How about you?"

"Oh, no. I'm stuffed, too. Maybe next time."

Despite Violet's objection, I insist on paying once we've reached the counter at the front of the restaurant and are attended by the friendly hostess who greeted us when we arrived.

As we walk across the uneven pavement toward the van, Violet pulls two peppermint patties out of her bag.

"Here," she says, handing one to me. "These are pure nostalgia, for me."

"Aww! Addie wrote about your mom buying these for you!" I say as I admire the silver foil-wrapped disc.

"Healthy? No. But sometimes you just enjoy and don't look back," Violet says, putting the whole chocolate into her mouth.

"Agreed," I reply with a chuckle.

"Did you want to go the long way back, and see if we can locate that fish camp for old time's sake?" Violet asks as we buckle our seatbelts.

"Actually, if you don't mind…" I begin. "I'd like to go the long way and ride by a *different* landmark."

"Sure," Violet replies. "Where to?" She puts the van into drive.

"I can't believe I'm saying this. I never, in a million years, thought I'd utter these words…but I'd like to go by my childhood home," I say, my mouth becoming dry.

"Oh, I'd love to see it!" she says. "Are you sure you're up for that?"

"No," I admit. "But it feels right, and it never has before."

"Alright, then. You tell me the way," Violet says as we inch toward the highway to Weatherford.

The wildly surreal drive to the old farmhouse I grew up in comes with a strong sense of familiarity, and a nervousness that builds the closer we get to the destination. I haven't been down the old country road since Daddy died, and haven't had a desire to, either

I'd resolved that I had to leave it behind and never return…until now. It's beyond my understanding why I should suddenly want to visit the old homeplace. The bittersweet memories are sure to wash over me and knock me winding, but still…I feel compelled to take Violet there.

My eyes begin to sting as we make our way down the curvy, country road I traveled nearly every day as a child. Sitting beside Daddy in the seat of the old blue pickup truck while he drove and dragged on Camel cigarettes, the sound of country music playing on the radio.

My heart races as we draw nearer to the old house, and I notice my breaths getting shaky.

I finally speak, breaking the deafening silence.

"Oh, this feels so strange. I can't even describe it," I utter as I stare out the window.

"I'll bet," Violet answers. "But, you know…maybe it'll feel good to come out here after all this time."

"I can promise you this…the Blaire from a couple of years back wouldn't have dreamed of doing this. I wouldn't have touched the idea with a ten-foot pole," I chortle. "I guess I've really healed better than I realized."

"I'm proud of you," Violet says as we slowly make our way past farms and fields.

"I guess I'm proud of me, too," I reply.

"Alright, we're getting close," I say, leaning forward in my seat. "Up ahead, on the left is what we're looking for. I guess, just creep past…I'm sure someone lives there."

As we approach the old familiar farm, my heart lurches in my chest. Our old mailbox is still standing, though severely dented by drunken vandals. Violet's van inches forward slowly, allowing me to behold the old home at the end of the dirt driveway.

"Hmm," she says. "I don't see any cars. It looks kind of abandoned, *doesn't* it?"

"Yeah, it does," I answer, closely studying the house and its surroundings.

"Turn in, if you don't mind."

Violet turns the van into the driveway, and we begin slowly toward the towering farmhouse whose white exterior has now become gray. Overgrown shrubs crowd the front porch, concealing a large portion of it. Unpruned branches stretch out across the side of the house, pointing to a broken window. Small trees have taken over the path that leads from the house to the near-collapsing barn.

Violet glances over at me as I cover my mouth in disbelief.

"So sad," I murmur, shaking my head.

"It's okay," Violet offers with a look of compassion.

My eyes begin to sting as I glance around the place. "What has happened to my home?" I finally say.

Violet stops the van in front of the house. "Do you want to get out?" she asks.

I shake my head, as the tears begin pouring.

"Maybe this wasn't such a great idea," I sputter.

I vaguely feel Violet's hand on my shaking shoulder as I weep into my palms. I was right not to come here before.

"It's okay, Blaire," Violet says calmly as she drums her fingers on my back.

Finally, I gain enough composure to speak between sniffles.

"Why did I do this to myself?"

"Do you want to leave?" Violet asks.

"No. Let's just sit here for a minute," I reply.

"Daddy used to park the truck right about here."

I dab my cheek with the sleeve of my sweater.

"Teenage Blaire would be sitting right here beside Daddy in the old pickup truck." I sniffle.

"We'd have just come from a cattle auction, where he didn't buy anything. It's Friday night, so we're in a hurry to get inside and turn the TV on *The Dukes of Hazzard.*" I manage a hoarse chuckle.

Violet seems to listen closely as I flash back to a time when there were no worries, only a simply jubilant life.

"The house would be filled with the smell of a fresh pound cake and coffee, while the Bunn coffee maker worked quickly to pump out the steamy, black liquid into the glass pot. Grandmama would already have little dessert plates and coffee cups sitting out on the table."

Violet offers a consoling pat on my shoulder. "I know it must be hard to see a place with so many nice memories abandoned like this," she says, looking up at the tattered farmhouse.

"It doesn't make any sense. I mean, the state took ownership of the house and land back when Daddy died. They'd have sold it, right?" I ask, confused.

"You'd think so," Violet answers. "I don't think they'd let it sit here and fall apart...maybe it *was* sold and whoever bought it passed away, or..." Violet shrugs.

"Yeah, I don't know. And why should I care? It's not like it's any of my concern anymore," I murmur, looking at my lap.

"Well, I think I know what you really need," Violet says with a cunning smile.

I turn to face her, waiting for her to continue.

"Me and the kids are leaving in the morning to go down to the coast for a few days. Mom had a beach house, which I inherited, and we go down just about every chance we get. Why don't you come along? I know it's the middle of Winter...but we still always enjoy ourselves. Plus, the beach so vacant and peaceful this time of year."

I manage a smile at the thought of Madge's beach house that Addie has mentioned so many times in her diaries.

"That really sounds wonderful," I admit. "But I'm supposed to work this weekend." I roll my teary eyes at the dreadful thought of my job.

"Darn. Well, maybe you could get out of it. Maybe there's someone who'd like to pick up some extra hours?"

"There *is* one person I could ask," I say, thinking of the part-time nurse named Mandy who appreciates extra hours.

"Then again, there's always the option to call in sick…" I raise an impish brow at the thought of playing hooky.

Violet giggles. "Sure, you could," she says.

"We'll see," I utter after a moment. "I'll let you know what I can arrange."

Though the excitement of possibly spending the weekend at the beach with Violet temporarily soothed my distress, it rears its ugly head again as we slowly back out of the dirt driveway. I sit facing the empty, old house one more time. It seems to reflect my own grief as it stands alone and on the verge of crumbling.

"We can stay as long as you want," Violet says gently.

"No, it's okay. I'm ready to go," I answer.

The long, winding country road back toward town seems even longer. My mind flashes back to my desolate home despite my efforts to reject the depressing thoughts.

"I hope you'll be able to go with us," Violet says as she drives. "If you really want to, that is."

"Oh, I *do* want to! I think you're right, in that it's just what I need. I haven't been to the beach in forever. It would be nice to get away for a few days."

"Well, let's cross our fingers that Mandy wants the hours…or that you decide to come down with a very short-lived illness," Violet says with a mischievous snicker.

~

It was a whirlwind of a day, trampling all over my emotions. From being so excited to have lunch with Violet at Addie and Madge's restaurant, to having the wind knocked out of me at the sight of my abandoned childhood home, to then being somewhat relieved at the idea of taking a beach trip with Violet…in Madge's beach cottage, no less.

Once Violet dropped me off this afternoon, I called Joseph and had a long conversation with him, although it wasn't so much a conversation as it was Joseph listening as I cried into the phone, telling him the sad and the happy details of my day. When I told him that Violet had invited me to spend a few days at the beach house, he encouraged me to go.

"Maybe it'll give you a chance to think things over about what you want…you know, with your job and everything," he'd said.

He always seems to know just what I need, even when I am unsure myself. But I think what I appreciate the most is knowing that the decision is all mine for the making.

As soon as I got off the phone with Joseph, I called Mandy from work to see if she would be interested in taking my weekend shifts. I had no idea what her response would be, but I was pleased to hear her accept the offer. I hadn't thought of a backup plan in case she'd said no, but I'd already made up my mind that I'd take the trip with Violet nonetheless.

Now, as I rummage around my bedroom in search of things to pack for the trip, I find I have to consciously repel thoughts of the old house from my mind. It lingers still, but I refuse to let it ruin my excitement for the upcoming weekend. There's nothing I can do about it anyway, as Joseph so candidly reminded me.

After packing a few outfits and toiletries, I saunter over to the bookcase and scan the row containing Addie's diaries. There's one left that I haven't read. That last diary feels like such a treasure as I reach for it. A wave of bittersweetness washes over me; I don't know what I'll do once I've read all of Addie's handwritten words. She has been such a comfort, reprieve, and teacher to me with the wonderful thoughts she wrote down.

I slowly take the diary from the shelf. The cover, adorned with hundreds of monarch butterflies, lies in wait for me to crack it open and absorb every last word. The spiral book looks old – the cover stiff and a bit faded. I take it to the suitcase lying open on my bed and carefully lay it on top of the folded clothing, before picking it back up again.

Wind and rain wisp by the opened drapes, sending leaves onto the large window as thunder rumbles in the distance. Sitting on the foot of the bed, I slowly turn the cover of the final diary. Just a few pages is all I need.

TEN

My spirit is troubled this evening. Though my life is wonderfully rich with the blessings of births and flavored with the rich multitudes of summer harvests, it is Madge that weighs on my mind today. It began when I went out to a local farm to pick up a couple of grocery items.

I had run out of bacon, which I always buy in bulk quantities from Charlie Whitfield. I made the drive out to his farm to see if he had any available for sale, and while I was there, I bought a few cucumbers from his warm-spirited little girl. Though I have plenty of them here in my own garden, I couldn't resist seeing the bubbling pride upon her little face as she made the sale.

I also saw one-half of what could be a family...if only Madge would tell. Every time I visit his farm, it takes every ounce of self-control not to break my promise to my dear Madge. Charlie deserves to know about little Violet. It seems cruelly unfair to rob that man of the knowledge of a second daughter. I've said everything short of begging, yet Madge won't hear of it. In her eyes, she's protecting him from shame as well as the financial burden of another child. She says she can love Violet just as well on her own, and that she just can't bring herself to interfere with his life or his livelihood.

So instead, she tells people that Violet's father, "her husband", died while she was with child. According to her, he fell asleep while driving a logging truck down the mountain and never woke up.

Like me, Madge mostly keeps to herself. Nobody questions her story or denies having known she had a husband to begin with, because not very many people even know Madge exists. She prefers it that way, and I can sympathize. I suppose that common thread is what drew the two of us together at the beginning of our friendship. But she knows that her self-contained lifestyle would come to an abrupt end, the minute it began buzzing around among the Weatherford community that Charlie Whitfield had another daughter. Though she may very well be correct, I simply cannot concur with her in this particular matter.

There's no use bothering her about it anymore, however. She has made up her mind, and I suppose it's final. Charlie hasn't the faintest idea that I know Madge, and it's best to keep it that way. Although I consider myself a woman of wisdom and self-control, I do fear that a slight slip of the tongue could happen by mistake, should he and I ever discuss Madge at any depth.

I just happen to believe that Charlie would see to it that Violet had a loving father. And from my view, he's already got that role thoroughly mastered.

From my dusty cutlass, I saw the blonde girl come running out of a farmhouse similar to my own and go skipping across the yard toward her father. After he'd scooped her up and held her against his sweat-stained, button-down shirt, he carefully sat her down where she played happily alongside him. I envisioned Violet next to them there. Though Madge is an exceptional mother, I am unable to repel the belief that Violet would greatly benefit from the addition of a sister and a father.

I suppose there's no use agonizing over things I cannot change. To be fair, it's not my business to be concerned with anyway, and it's certainly not my business to meddle in. Besides, Madge has given me permission to use her beach cottage this week, as I have no mothers due to give birth anytime soon. Madge says she will be glad to tend to my farm animals, as well. I must come up with something special to repay her. I just feel the need for a little change of scenery for a few days. I will, of course, pack my beloved diary along with the small suitcase full of things I have prepared by the front door.

All there is to do now is brew my evening cup of tea and retire to the front porch while the orange sun slowly slips behind the mountain. The warm, pink-tinted outdoors is sure to welcome me with a glowing, streaked sky and a triumphant song sung by the crickets and cicadas. The air will be scented with sage and gardenia. The honeybees will be flying to bed, and I'll shortly follow suit. Tomorrow evening will surely find me barefoot on the soft sand of the beach, collecting seashells in the breezy, salty air.

From the author

If you've read the first book in this series, 'The Primrose of Bascomb', you might've noticed the slow, steady conversion Blaire is now making toward a different way of life. Little by little, her former life, including her job, begins to look unappealing to her. She meets Violet, who may indirectly influence the growth toward a different course for her life.

During our lives as Christians, we all experience the conversion period to establishing a new, more meaningful way of life, and it can be a scary one. Oftentimes, new believers are unsure of what to do next in their life-long journey. These times call for those positive influences, to act as a guide...to positively influence the growth toward a different course of life.

I personally have a hard time being a "people person". While, yes, I love people with a conscious effort , I don't have the outstanding personality that others are easily drawn to. But I have to remind myself often that it doesn't really matter what comes easily to me and what doesn't. We are called to not only love one *another, **but also** to make disciples. Are you in a season of needing a leader to nurture your growth in Christ, or are you in a phase of urging others toward a life that glorifies Him?*

My prayer is that you have the support here on Earth to make your walk a little less wobbly.

Titus 2:3-5